STARFISH

LISA FIPPS

STAR FISH

THORNDIKE PRESS
A part of Gale, a Cengage Company

GALE
A Cengage Company

LIBRARY OF CONGRESS CIP DATA ON FILE.
CATALOGUING IN PUBLICATION FOR THIS BOOK
IS AVAILABLE FROM THE LIBRARY OF CONGRESS.

ISBN-13: 978-1-4328-9096-4 (hardcover alk. paper)

Published in 2021 by arrangement with Nancy Paulsen Books, an imprint of Penguin Young Readers Group, a division of Penguin Random House LLC.

Printed in Mexico
Print Number : 3   Print Year : 2022

*To every kid who's ever been told,
"You'd be so pretty or handsome,
if . . ." You ARE beautiful. Now. Just as
you are. You deserve to be seen, to be
heard, to take up room, to be noticed.
So when the world tries to make you
feel small, starfish!*

FOR JUST A WHILE

I step down into the pool.
The water is bathwater warm
but feels cool
compared to the blisteringly hot air.
Kick. Gliiiiiiide.
Stroke. Gliiiiiiide.
Side to side
and back again.
Dive under the surface.
Soar to the top.
Arch my back.
Flip. Flop.

As soon as I slip into the pool,
I am weightless.
Limitless.
For just a while.

Name-Calling

Eliana Elizabeth Montgomery-Hofstein.
That's my name.

My bestie, Viv,
and my parents call me
Ellie or El.

But most people call me Splash

or some synonym for *whale*.

Cannonball into a pool,
drenching everyone,
and wear a whale swimsuit
to your Under the Sea birthday party
when you're a chubby kid
who grows up to be a fat tween
and no one will ever let you live it down.

Ever.

Splash Is Born

Now, whenever I swim,
I use the steps to ease into the water,
careful not to make waves,
because the memory
of my pool party plays
in my head like a video on a loop.

It was my fifth birthday.
I wanted to be the first one in, so
I ran to the edge and
leapt into the air and
tucked my knees into my chest.

Water sprayed up
as I sank down.
I bobbed to the surface,
expecting cheers for
the splashiest cannonball ever.

That didn't happen.

"Splash spawned a tsunami!"
my sister, Anaïs, shouted.
"She almost emptied the pool,"
my brother, Liam, chimed in.
I dove under,
drowning my tears.

I wish I could tell everyone
how they made me feel that day —
humiliated,
angry,
deeply sad.

But every time I try to stand up for
myself,
the words get stuck in my throat
like a giant glob of peanut butter.

Besides, if they even listened,
they'd just snap back,
"If you don't like being teased,
lose weight."

FAT GIRL RULES

Some girls my age fill
diaries with dreams and
private thoughts.

Mine has a list of
Fat Girl Rules.

You find out
what these unspoken rules are
when you break them —
and suffer
the consequences.

Fat Girl Rules
I learned
at five:
No cannonballs.
No splashing.
No making waves.

You don't deserve
to be seen or heard,
to take up room,
to be noticed.

Make yourself small.

WHAT, WHY, WHO, HOW, WHEN

The first Fat Girl Rule
you learn hurts the most,
a startling, scorpion-stinging soul slap.

Something's changed, but you don't
   know
what.
You replay the moment in your mind from
every possible angle, trying to understand
why.
Why the rules exist and
who.
Who came up with them and
how.
How does anyone have the right to tell
   you
how to live just because of your weight?

Mostly, you remember the smack of
the change.
One minute you were like
everybody else, playing around, enjoying
   life,
and then,
with the flip of an unseen cosmic switch,
you're the fat girl,
stumbling,
trying to regain your balance.
Acting as if you know what you're doing,
   like
when
you used to play dress-up
and tried to walk
in high-heeled shoes.

THE GIFT

Every time I see a pudgy preschooler,
I want to hand her my list,
like the answer sheet for a test,
to spare her the pain of learning
the rules firsthand.

But instead,
I give each girl the gift
of more days,
weeks,
and months
of a normal life.

Whatever that is.

BELLIES DANCING

Viv's mom caught her dad with
another woman and said Texas
wasn't big enough for the three of them.
So now my best friend has to move
to Indiana.

In my backyard, we livestream
the Latin Music Festival
on an outdoor screen
as part of her going-away party.

Viv starts belly dancing
like she learned in a class at
the Dallas Public Library,
where her mom was a librarian.
I follow her lead and
our arms morph into snakes
as our hips figure-eight.

My dog, Gigi, a pug,
runs circles around us as
we sing at the top of our lungs
along with the bands and
dance with complete abandon,
like you do when you're alone in your
  room
trying out some new moves
or making up some of your own.

Except it turns out
we're not
alone.

THE NEW NEIGHBOR

Mid-twirl, I open my eyes to see
a girl's head pop up over the fence,
then disappear and reappear.

This trampoline girl
saw me shake parts of me
I didn't even know I had.

"What do you think you're doing?"
I stop dancing so fast
I about give myself whiplash.

I see her head again.
"IheardDíasDivertidos."
She says it so quickly it's like one word.
She disappears and reappears.

"Couldn'thelpmyself."
In a flash,
she climbs over the fence
and lands in front of me.
"I'm Catalina Rodriguez."

A Poet and a Musician

Catalina points to the concert on the
  screen.
"Wow! So you like Días Divertidos, too?
I have all their songs on my playlist."

"Me too," I say.

"Who else do you listen to?"

"Don't get Ellie started."
Viv rolls her eyes.
If eye-rolling were an Olympic sport,
she'd be a gold medalist.

"I'm a poet, so
I love music because
lyrics are sung poems," I say.
"Rap and country are my faves."

"I'm a guitarist," Catalina says.
"I like all music but love Latin."

She chooses her words carefully, like me.
But she's not like me.
Catalina's skinny
like a pancake.
I'm more like a three-tiered cake.

My fatdar should be sounding the alarm.
Why isn't it?

The Thing about Fatdar

Fatdar is a lot like
Spider-Man's Spidey sense,
a sixth sense.

Somehow we just know when
someone's about to say
something hurtful or
do something mean.

Even in a crowd,
I can spot a fatphobe,
someone who's grossed out
by overweight people.
Fatphobes give off this vibe.
Part discomfort.
Part shock.
Part fear.
Part anger.

And all hatred.

SHADOWS

"'Baila conmigo'!"
Catalina shouts as the next song starts
and she dances with us.

"Teach me that one move, Ellie," she
    says.
"Which one?"
"The one where you were
kinda kicking your leg
while you spun."

When I dance
knowing Catalina's watching,
I feel every pound of my legs,
see my fat shake,
and notice how round
my shadow on the grass is
next to her angles,
so I stop.

Fat Girl Rule:
Move slowly so
your fat doesn't jiggle,
drawing attention to your body.

But that uncomfortable-in-my-own-skin
  feeling
fades as the music blares
and Catalina squeal-screams,
going all bananas with us,
during the tribute to Selena.

If dance partners were food,
Catalina and I would be
peanut butter and jelly.
Cookies and milk.
Chips and salsa.
We're different, but
make a perfect combo,
heads, hips, and hands
moving in sync.

Right on cue as the sun sets,
the katydids start their singing,
fast and furious since

their tempo's based on heat
or maybe Selena's *bidi-bidi-bom-bom*
  beat.

"Catalina, dale las buenas noches
y ven a casa," a woman's voice calls out.
"Gotta go," Catalina tells us.
"Thanks for letting me crash your party."

She climbs back over the fence,
then trampolines.
"Can'twaittocomeoveragain."

LIKE PICASSO

Some people have mood rings.
Viv has mood hair.
You can always tell how she's feeling
based on her hair color.
Since she has to move,
she's like Picasso
— in a blue period.

Her bottom lip juts out
as she pouts,
and when she huffs,
her stick-straight blond bangs
with blueberry tips
stand straight up for a second.

"What's wrong?"
I ask when we float in the pool,
cooling off after the concert.

"Today was our last day together
until who knows when
and not only did I have to share you,
but I also had to watch while
you made a new friend."

New friend?
Catalina?
Is she?

SAYING GOODBYE

The stars at night
might be big and bright
deep in the heart of Texas,
but not where we live,
thanks to light pollution.

"Sirius."
I point to the brightest star, the only
   visible one.
"Leave it to you to know the dog star."
"Notice there are no cat stars."

"Maybe not in the Milky Way," Viv says,
"but I'm sure there's a galaxy
— more evolved than ours —
where cats rule.
They'll invade our planet
and make all pugs prisoners.

Admit you'll miss Oreo."
She splashes me with each syllable.

"Only if you admit you'll miss Gigi."
I splash back.

When Viv's mom picks her up,
we promise to text, video-chat —
whatever it takes to stay connected.
Viv suggests we make a blood oath.
I remind her she faints when she sees one
    drop.
We settle for a tame, lame pinky swear.
Viv starts to open the car door,
but then throws her arms around me.

We cry our goodbyes.

SUPER SLEUTH

Every kid needs one place
they can escape to when
life gets to be too much.

The pool is my place.

Today I've been in the water so long,
my fingers look like raisins,
but I plan to swim and float for hours
   more,
mourning my first day without Viv
and the last day of summer vacation.

"Ilovetoswim.
CanIjoinyou?"
Catalina's back on the trampoline.

I barely know her,
so can I trust her
with the pool?

I haven't swum
with anyone
but Viv since
the Under the Sea party.

I still don't know why
Catalina wants to hang around me.
Could she be friends with
Marissa and Kortnee and
helping them set me up for a prank?

I climb out of the pool and
wrap my towel around my
shoulders like a superhero cape.

Time to activate my sleuth powers.

"I wish I could keep swimming,
but I have to get my stuff ready
for school tomorrow."
I don't lie.

Catalina climbs over the fence.
"I've been putting it off, too.
I dread being the new girl."

Like Wonder Woman with her lasso,
I seek truth.

I ask Catalina,
"You going to go to Kiser Academy?"

"Is that where you go, Ellie?"

I nod.

"I wish. Then we'd be together.
But I'm going to Bishop Joseph Catholic
    School."

Wonder Woman wouldn't give up
until she had all the answers.
Neither can I.
"Wanna get our stuff ready together?"

"I thought you'd never ask."

A Fresh Start

The best part of
going back to school
is the back-to-school supplies.

We dump everything on the floor.
Catalina zooms in on one of my prized
   finds:
flamingo pens with feathers.
"Watch what happens when you write," I
   say.
The flamingo dances
as I scribble on a piece of paper.

She trades me a unicorn pen for one.
It lights up when she taps it.
"Great for writing in bed.
The best ideas for songs come at night."

"Same with poems!
Viv and I used to do this,
swap and share supplies."

"Me and my friends, too,
but they're all back in Houston."

So she's not from here.
She doesn't know Marissa and Kortnee.
She doesn't know I'm Splash.
Being friends with her will be like
opening a brand-new notebook,
a clean, fresh start.

LUCKY DOG

Every morning,
my pug stands on her hind legs,
snatching kibble out of the scoop
before I even have a chance
to dump the food into her bowl.

Gigi doesn't hide her hunger.
She feels pure joy
when eating.

She devours every bite
and licks the bowl.

Her tummy full,
she circles three times before
lying down and
resting her chin on my feet
under the breakfast table.

Curled up and cozy,
she soon starts snoring.

She's happy with her round body.
Content.
Comfortable.

And no one bullies her because of it.

Lucky dog.

FAMILY FOR BREAKFAST

We have a family tradition
of eating
breakfast and dinner all together
on the first day of school.

No exceptions.

"Grub's ready."
Dad slides omelets and toast onto plates.

"But scrambled egg whites or oatmeal
was what we'd agreed."
Mom talks like a ventriloquist,
through her teeth with her lips fake smiling.

I surrender my food to Liam,
who'll be a junior in high school this year,
and make a beeline for the fridge
for some fat-free yogurt
that's yet to make me fat-free.

A new article dangles from a refrigerator
   magnet:
"Dairy Products Might Aid Weight Loss."
It slightly covers the other articles,
including my fave:
"Tips to Be a Real Loser."
Mom just loves hanging these articles
on the fridge for me.
She's a writer and magazine editor,
but spins her words for a different reason
   than I.

I plan to become a storyteller,
and a poet,
to help people feel what it's like
to live in
someone else's skin.

Mom's a journalist,
determined to expose
all that's wrong in the world
and spotlight everyone's flaws,
not caring if she
gets under people's skin.

DOES SHE REMEMBER?

Dad looks at Anaïs and Liam.
Both are wearing new clothes.
I tug on the hem of my
old button-down shirt,
trying to make it longer.

"No new clothes for Ellie?" Dad asks
    Mom.

"She gained more weight this summer.
I'm afraid if we keep buying her bigger
    clothes,
she'll just let herself *get* bigger."

If Mom thinks I look horrible now,
wait until I can't fit in anything — and
have to go naked.

Liam inhales his food
and belches, "I'm outta here."

Seconds later, the back door slams,
and tires squeal as he shows off
his red Mustang.
He thinks he's a stallion since he's
    sixteen.

"Enjoy sixth grade, Splash,"
Anaïs calls over her shoulder as she
    leaves
to start her senior year of high school.
That's like saying to a shark bite victim,
"Enjoy the free liposuction."

I wonder if my sister even remembers
it's her fault
everyone calls me Splash,
how that one word
on one day
changed my world.

LIFE ON A TEETER-TOTTER

Dealing with my parents is like
riding a teeter-totter nonstop.

Dad promises me a shopping spree.
Up I go.

"Good luck finding anything she can
   wear."
Down I go.

"We'll do just fine without you."
Up I go.

Mom grabs her briefcase, purse, and
   keys.
"Just don't forget El's first appointment
with the therapist."

Down I go.
Fast.
Hard.

41

Like when the other person
jumps off the teeter-totter and
throws everything off-balance.
"Huh? Wait. What?"

Mom's shoulders droop as
one hand freezes on the doorknob.
"You said you'd tell her."
She shoots eye daggers at Dad.

He shoos her away like an annoying fly.
"Go on. I've got this."

The whale has to go to a shrink?
It's a punch line for a bad fat joke.

JUDASED

Dad rips the weight-loss articles off the
  fridge
and tosses them into the trash.
"I'm sorry you found out this way."
He says he never got around
to talking to me about the therapist
because he'd been swamped with
  work —
but then he goes on and on about
the importance of talking.

Do parents ever hear themselves?

"You're a psychiatrist, Dad.
I talk to you all the time."

Dad straddles the chair next to me.
"It's not the same thing.
Your mom and I agree

Dr. Wood could help you."
Translation?
Mom nagged, and Dad caved.

"Judasssssss!"
I hiss the s like
a western diamondback rattlesnake.
Dad's always had my back.
Not the knife in it.

THE LESSER OF TWO DEVILS

I don't ride the bus.
Dad takes me.
When we turn the final corner
and I can see the school,
my stomach somersaults;
it's the only part of me
that can do gymnastics.

I text Viv.
I really need her,
especially after that
freaking family breakfast.

Don't know if I can do this alone,
   Viv.
I'm freaking out.

Just chill.

I'm tryin'.
It's just — ugh.
I add a string of emojis.
Frowny face.
Worried face.
Sad face.

I know.
I know.
She adds a hug emoji.
But if I can do it, so can you.
After all, I've gotta go to
a whole new school.
Remember, the devil you do know
is better than the devil you don't!

Yeah. But they're both devils.

H-E-Double-Hockey-Stick

Happy Monday, Dallas!
the radio deejay yells over the airwaves
as Dad pulls into the drop-off lane.
Gonna hit one hundred and ten!
Perfect weather to hang out by the pool.

I wish.

"Okay, Ellie. Have a good day at —"
I slam the door,
cutting Dad off.

As he pulls away,
I hear someone singing
"Baby Beluga."
I don't have to turn around to know
it's Marissa.

And so it begins.

Giggles.
Stares.
Rejection.

The devils I do know.

Kortnee holds open the door — until I
    head in.
It slams, nearly smashing my face.
"Oopsie!"
she yells over her shoulder.

Even without the scorching Texas sun,
I am officially in
h-e-double-hockey-stick.

PRETEND-IOUS PRETENTIOUS

While conjugating verbs in French class,
I imagine Viv
at her new school and
figure I stink
because I don't want to think
of her making new friends.

To punish myself,
I conjugate the present tense of *puer*
from *I stink* (Je pue) to
They stink (Ils/elles puent).

The lunch bell rings.
Thanks to Chef Brigitte at Kiser Café,
gourmet food is on the menu every day,
as in artichoke pizza on wheat flatbread
 or
veggie burger with Moroccan cilantro
 spread.

Chef? Oh, yes. A chef.
A cafeteria worker simply won't do,
nor will the word *cafeteria*.
Mais non!
Our private school's too classy,
uses français
to make everything from *aah* to *zed*
  sound good.

But let's call it what it is.
School lunch is for bullies
to dine on their prey.

Bon appétit.

HUNGRY GAMES

I stare down the hallway,
Katnissing in the Hungry Games,
wanting nothing more than to get out
    alive.

I spot muttations —
part piranha with their gnashing teeth,
part wolverine with their claws,
and part hyena with their howling
    laughter
— posing as students.

I'm hungry for escape.
They're hungry for laughs.
And there's no way out but through the
    arena.

"Get back! Make room! Thar she blows!"
A guy sucks in his stomach

and slams back against the hallway wall
as if my blubber takes up all the room.
Viv and I call him
Enemy Number 3,
ranking behind
Enemy Number 1, Marissa,
and Enemy Number 2, Kortnee.

The sea of students parts
as everyone crashes left or right
to hug the hallways.
It happens every day.
Every day since first grade.

Ils puent.

LIFESAVING LIBRARIANS

The library is my safe harbor since
I dare not go into the cafeteria alone,
a whale surrounded by starving sharks.
It was hard enough when
Viv and I faced them together.

"How'd your summer reading go, El?"
Mrs. Pochon asks.

I tell the librarian about my new favorite
novels in free verse.

"Imagine that, eh?"
Her Canadian accent is strong.
"Poetry at the top of your list."
She smiles as she scans a book,
its spine snapping and plastic jacket
    crackling.

I breathe in the smell,
hungry to read the words.

"You'll like this one," she says.
"I've been looking forward to seeing you
so you could check it out."

She's the first person to smile at me
  today.
The first to make me feel wanted.
Understood.
I blink back tears.
It's unknown how many students' lives
librarians have saved
by welcoming loners at lunch.

SMOWNING

Wind chimes dangling from the door
bang and clang,
announcing my arrival at
the dollhouse-sized office with
its living room turned waiting room and
sunroom turned therapy room, which
is all so fitting for
my life turned nightmare.

Dishes rattle in a sink somewhere and
a voice calls out,
"Make yourself comfortable
in my office, Ellie.
Join you in a minute."

"That's Dr. Wood," Dad says,
taking off his cowboy hat
and sitting down in the waiting room.
You can take the man out of the ranch,

55

but you can't take the ranch out of the
    man.
"You'll like her."
He winks and
draws up one side of his mouth and
makes a double click.
I call it his cowboy charmer.
"Trust me."

"Not anymore I don't."
Venom drips from my voice as
I give him an exaggerated smile
that quickly morphs into a frown —
the *smown*, we call it.

I'm famous for them.

POWER STRUGGLE

I decide to go
toe to toe
with Dr. Woodn't-You-Like-to-Know.

When she comes into the office,
she finds me in her chair,
throwing her off her game,
taking away a smidge of her power.

She purses her lips.
"Hmm."
Then she sits on the couch.
"Ellie, tell me why you're here."

My therapist is skin and bones.
Couldn't they at least
have found a fat one
who might
understand me?

I fold my arms across my chest,
the universal sign for *conversation closed*.
I may have no choice about being here,
but I can choose if and when I talk.

"You do realize seeing a therapist
is about having someone to talk to,
to sort out what's going on in your life
and how you feel about it,
to figure out what you can do
to change or accept it.
It's nothing to be ashamed or afraid of."
Dr. Woodn't-You-Like-to-Know
raises her eyebrows,
forming wavy forehead wrinkles.

She's paid to put up with me,
so I show a little sass.
"I know.
My dad's a psychiatrist, remember?"

Eyes roll.
Mine.
Then hers.

"Not in the mood to talk today, huh?
That's fine."

She scribbles on a pad
until time's up.
With each word she writes,
she takes back her power.

I wish I could smart off
to my parents like I did to
Dr. Woodn't-You-Like-to-Know,
tell them what I really think,
especially Mom,
but I guess I'm too scared
of how she'll react.
She makes life hard enough now,
while I'm keeping my thoughts to myself.

Why aren't kids allowed
to tell grown-ups when they're wrong?

They don't know
everything.

Sometimes it's as if
they don't know
anything.

CHOICES — FINALLY

"While you were with Dr. Wood,
I texted Aunt Zoey, and she told me
about a new boutique
for plus-size kids and teens."

"Whatever."

At my size,
shopping for clothes isn't fun.
I just want
what everyone else my age wears,
to blend in,
since I already stand out.
But it's hardly ever in my size.

At least shopping with Dad
is way better than with Mom.
She always tells me to try on clothes
that won't even fit over my head

and then kvetches
that I need to stick to my diet.
Mom always says,
"You'd be so pretty"
— and all the big girls in the world
can finish this sentence in unison —
"if you lost weight."

After the boutique owner, Diana,
introduces herself and
welcomes us,
Dad says,
"I'll be over there reading."
He points to a lounge area.
He always has a book with him.
"You just have three rules right now,
   Ellie.
Enjoy.
No limits.
Take your time."

My eyes lock onto
an orange peasant top with
embroidered turquoise flowers,
my two favorite colors.

At first I think it's probably not in my
   size.
But I discover it is.
Everything is!
I've never had so many
cool clothes to choose from.

Or had a store like this to shop in.
Even the mannequins here
are my size.

I'm Charlie in the chocolate factory.

FEELING PRETTY

"I love your store.
I don't know where to start!"
I tell Diana.

"Thanks.
I've dreamed of having
a shop like this since
I was your age."
Diana leans on a display near me
as I search the racks of shirts and jeans.
"You're lucky," she says.
"Finding plus-size clothes is easier now.
When I was young,
clothes for zaftigs were just ugh."
She places one hand on her neck,
as if the memories strangle her.

63

Zaftig means "pleasantly plump."
It comes from
the Yiddish word *zaftik*.

Bobeshi spoke Yiddish
all the time,
so I know that word.

But no positive word for *fat*
would ever be in Mom's vocabulary.

"So my mom learned to sew," Diana
    continues.
"She created patterns just for my body."

I feel a twinge of envy
thinking about having a mom like hers,
someone who accepts us
and adapts the world to fit us,
instead of trying to make us
fit in the world.

Every time I get a chance,
I glance at Diana and
notice things about her.
Like how she wears
an off-the-shoulder shirt and short skirt

to show off her curves
— instead of hiding
as much of her body as possible,
like I do.

How she wears bright yellow
— instead of a dark color.

How she walks with confidence,
head held high,
happy to be seen
— instead of looking down at the floor,
like I do.

I want to be more like Diana.
Free to be me.
A zaftig.

I wish I were an octopus
as I shop.
Two arms can't hold
all the clothes I want.

For the first time,
I find things that make me feel

pretty.

I'm a Starfish

When I get back home from
Diana's boutique,
I try something new.

The pool's always been my escape.
The place I feel weightless
in today's fat-obsessed world.
I swim each morning and
try to hold on to that feeling
throughout the day.
But by the time school's over,
I feel every pound, plus
the added weight of shame
from all the comments and pranks.
The pool helps wash it all away.

Now I want the pool to be something
  more,
not only a place to escape,
but also a place to express myself.

As I float,
I spread out my arms
and my legs.
I'm a starfish,
taking up all the room I want.

FRIENDS, NOT ENEMIES

Boxes surround Viv as we video-chat.
"Are you packing up and
heading back here, where you belong?"

"Still unpacking here in Podunk."

Viv says her new public school has more
fat people than Kiser Academy,
so she's feeling at home.
I'm happy for her.

When she asks how my day went,
I tell her about all the bullying
and the therapist.

"No freakin' way!"
"No freakin' way what?"
her mom, Sue, asks,
bending over the screen to say hi,
so she's upside down to me.

After Viv fills her in, Sue says,
"Don't let your mom's issues with weight
become your issues with weight, kiddo."

"Stop hijacking our conversation!"
Viv playfully pushes her mom away.

I like how they act like best friends,
not mother and daughter.
Not archenemies like Mom and me.

After Sue leaves the room, Viv asks,
"But really. Why is everyone so mean to
  us?"

"Don't you know they're 'just joking'?"

"People laugh at jokes," Viv says.
"They shouldn't make us want
to go home and cry our eyes out.
What can we do about it, though?"

"How about we sit on them?"

Viv laughs at my tired joke until she cries.

I join her, and our tears
have nothing to do
with laughter.

Unappetizing

For dinner, I'm the appetizer.

"How'd it go with Dr. Wood?"
Mom starts in, even before
the first piece of steak reaches my
    mouth.

"Epic fail. She's fat as ever," Liam says.

"That's enough,"
Dad scolds my brother,
after waiting a beat,
like he often does
so Mom can say something in my
    defense.
But she never, ever does.

Anaïs catches my attention,
glances at Liam, and rolls her eyes,
as if saying, *What an idiot.*

That's nice for once.
Usually she laughs along with him,
but lately she seems annoyed with him, too.

Mom chews on her lips
more than her food,
as if she's biting back words.

"Hope you'll give Dr. Wood a chance."
Kale dangles from Mom's fork.

I nod.

She bites her lips again.
" 'Cause if therapy doesn't work,
we'll have to think of
s — something else, okay?"

She started to say something else, all right.
A word that begins with s.
Surgery.
Bariatric surgery.

I chew, chew, and chew,
but it seems like the piece of steak
grows larger,
so I secretly spit it into a napkin.

I've lost my appetite.

MISSING DAD

You can miss someone
even when they're with you.

It's storming,
and I'm bored.
I bounce through the house and
see Dad camped out
on the couch in his office.

I'd challenge him to a
backgammon battle,
if he hadn't Judased me
by siding with Mom about
me needing a therapist.

I inch backward
to return to my room
and avoid him,
but the wooden floor squeaks,
rats me out.

"Can't avoid me forever."

At the sound of Dad's voice,
Gigi hops onto his lap
and rolls over for a tummy rub.
She forgives him.

My dog's a better person than me.

SOMEONE TO TALK TO

Dad talks first.
"Still mad at me, I see."

"Just tell me why
you let Mom talk you into
making me go to a therapist."

"Dr. Wood was my idea."

"What? Are you kidding me, Dad?
I thought you were on my side!
I thought I could trust you!
I thought you loved me!"

"Sit down and hear me out."
"But —"
He points to the cushion.
"I'm not askin'."

I flop down.
Gigi senses something's wrong and

snorts at Dad before she comes over
and snuggles next to me.

At least my dog is still loyal.

"For a while your mom's pushed for
you to have surgery,
but I think you're way too young.
I've pushed for therapy because
I see the hurt in your eyes
from what people say and do to you."

Tears well up in my eyes.
Dad's noticed.
He cares.
Why hasn't Mom?

"It breaks my heart, Ellie.
I just think it'd be good for you
to have someone to talk to
about it all."

"But if therapy doesn't help me
lose the weight, then —"

"No surgery.
I promise.
If I'm lyin', may Oklahoma beat Texas
in every Red River Showdown until I die."

Ever since the first time
Mom said the word *surgery*,
it's as if fear-filled balloons
have been lodged in my lungs,
keeping me from taking a full breath.
With Dad's promise, they pop.

I can breathe again.

WHAT'S WRONG WITH HER?

I'm trying to fall asleep,
but my mind is a frozen computer.
It won't shut down.

I think of Nana Montgomery's story
about the night I was born.

While Mom was pregnant with me,
she had a premonition that
something was wrong.
So when they nestled me in her arms,
instead of cuddling me
and welcoming me into the world,
she just kept saying,
"What's wrong with her?
I know there's something wrong!
What is it?
Just tell me!"

Nothing has really changed
since then.
As an editor who prefers
to copyedit with red pen on paper,
Mom makes articles crisper, tighter,
  leaner.
And when she's unhappy with an
  article —
when she can't fix it and
it's beyond hope —
she puts a giant *X* on it.

If I were an article,
she'd put a giant *X* on me.

Hard to Fit In

"How was school today?"
Catalina asks as she climbs over the fence
with her guitar slung over her shoulder.

I let out a heavy sigh,
the kind where your lips
flutter like a motorboat.

"That good, huh?"

"Yours?"

"It's hard to fit in when
you're the new kid."

"I hear you.
It's hard to fit in when
you're the fat kid, too."

"Well, at least we have each other.
That's something."

We don't say a word,
yet we understand each other.

A friend hears what you say with silence.

Catalina strums her guitar,
playing softly
while I write
in my journal.

Pulling Sneakies

Everyone in my family plays the piano
— except me.
Years ago, I asked Mom for lessons
as a Christmas gift.

I remember joining her on the piano
  bench,
sliding my fingers over the slick, shiny
  keys.

"You really want to learn?" Mom asked.
"More than anything," I told her.
"Fine," she told me, and stood up and
  shut the lid.
"When you lose weight."

So now I never let Mom know what I
  want
because she'll keep it from me

as punishment for being fat
disguised as motivation to lose weight.

I write in my journal.
Fat Girl Rule my mom taught me:
If you're fat,
there are things
you can't have.

But Mom doesn't know
I can play a few songs
on the piano.
Nana Montgomery taught me.
"Let's pull a sneaky,"
Nana would say
when I stayed with her.
Pulling a sneaky meant
doing something Mom didn't allow.

I remember
Nana's wrinkled hands
positioning mine to play
"All You Need Is Love"
by the Beatles,
the rhythm slow
yet bouncy and fun,

and full of simple happiness
just like the joy
we felt while singing and playing
together.

And I remember her words
after every lesson.
"No matter what others say or do,
embrace what makes you, you."

I finish my writing and look up at
    Catalina,
who strums the last notes
of her song.

"How 'bout something cold to drink?"
I ask her.

"I could use a break from the heat,
that's for sure," she says.

As we dance our way to the kitchen,
Nana's words repeat in my head
like another song.

No matter what others say or do,
embrace what makes you, you.

TAKING INVENTORY

While Gigi slurps
at her water bowl,
I pour iced tea
for Catalina and me.

My stomach growls.
I'm tempted to eat
string cheese or
celery or
something like that.
But even eating a healthy snack
is a crime
for a fat girl.

I don't offer Catalina anything,
which feels rude,
but Mom will get mad,
thinking I ate it.

84

Like a police detective
hot on the trail of a hardened criminal,
Mom goes through the trash,
looking for evidence
that I've cheated on my latest diet.
Bags.
Wrappers.
Boxes.

And she inventories the food.
I found out the hard way years ago
when she barged into my bedroom
and freaked out on me.
"You're not supposed to be snacking.
Eating a few crackers would be
bad enough, but half a package?
No one needs that many saltines!"

I was still chewing,
and she grabbed the trash basket.
"Spit it out! Now!"
But the salt made my mouth so dry,
I couldn't.

"Dad! Dad! Come quick!"
Anaïs yelled as she and Liam watched.

85

Dad came in just in time to see
Mom try to pry my mouth open,
determined to remove every crumb,
as if I'd swallowed poison.

Then my parents had
one of their biggest fights ever.

Liam slipped a note under my door that
  night.
If they split up,
it's all your fault.
Hope the stupid crackers were worth it.

I haven't eaten saltines since.

Peacekeeper

Most every weekend I make time for
temple *and* church.
I'm Jewish because of Dad and
Christian because of Mom.

They taught us about both faiths
when we were young,
and then let us choose our own
when we were ready.

Anaïs and Liam chose Judaism.
But I chose both religions.
It's part of my self-imposed
peacekeeping mission, since
I already cause
a whale-sized rift
between my parents.

SECRET STASH

In the ripped-open side of a stuffed
  animal.
In the pockets of an old backpack.
In a hollowed-out book.
These are just a few
of my secret hiding places
where I stash food.

Years ago, one of Mom's diets for me
left me starving.
My stomach grumbled,
my hands shook,
and the room spun as
my body demanded more food.

Viv unknowingly rescued me by
inviting me for a sleepover.
Her mom baked cookies.

I snarfed several and
snatched three to sneak home.

When I got there,
I ripped out some stitches
on an old teddy bear
and tucked the cookies inside.

Ever since then,
every chance I get,
I squirrel away food.

I feel powerful and powerless,
free and bound,
all at the same time.

TUG-OF-WAR

It's never a good sign when
they pick the fat girl first in gym.

We're playing tug-of-war.

War is a fitting name since
middle school's one big battlefield.
"I guess it pays
to have a lard butt around sometimes,"
Marissa says as she ties the anchor loop
around my waist.
My fellow teammates laugh.

"No fair!"
Kortnee yells from the other end of the
    rope.
"Splash could anchor a navy ship."

Kortnee's team cheats,
tugs even before

90

the PE teacher blows the whistle.
Several people in front of me aren't
  ready,
and we all
fall
like dominoes.

I feel the anchor rope tighten around me
as Kortnee's team drags me across the
  floor.

"Heave-ho, the whale must go.
Heave-ho, the whale must go."
Kortnee starts the chant and
soon the words echo throughout the
  gym.

This is how I'm going to die —
with people laughing at me —
same as how I've lived.

Surely, someone sees me struggling.
Yet no one stops the war to help me.
Not even the teacher.

When Kortnee's team wins,
I remove the rope and

relief floods my body,
until Marissa and some teammates
come over and yell at me
for making them big fat losers
like me.

TAKE TWO

I find Dr. Woodn't-You-Like-to-Know
planted as firmly in her chair
as cotton in the South Plains.
Touché.
I sit on the couch.

"Ellie, would you share
something that happened today?"

Like the near-death tug-of-war?
Or when Marissa posted on social media
a picture of me eating a cupcake at
the library's Banned Books Week
   celebration,
along with the poll question,
"Ban fatties from cupcakes, yes or no?"
I didn't have to guess the results.

I say nothing.
Instead, I play a silent game of I spy,
trying to figure out the therapist.
Dr. Woodn't-You-Like-to-Know
shelves books based on color,
not alphabetically,
so I think she obviously can't be trusted.
But then I spy
picture frames scattered about
showing her friends of all shapes.

Maybe I can trust her — a little.

DOGGONE GOOD TRICK

"Ellie, do you mind if
my dog joins us today?
It's okay if you do mind."

"Mind?
Heck no.
I prefer dogs over humans."

"I'll try not to be offended by that,"
Dr. Woodn't-You-Like-to-Know says,
    and smiles.

When her border collie enters the office
and jumps up on me as if he's
the size of my pug instead of a pony,
I'm tempted to make a joke about
Dr. Woodn't-You-Like-to-Know's
practice going to the dogs.

I check his collar: *Patches*.
"Quite a fitting name with your
patches of black and white.
And look at those icy blue eyes.
Reminds me of my mom's.
Well, her blue eye.
She has one blue, one brown.
Heterochromia.
It's genetic."

I think about how genes can make you
more likely to be fat, too.

Mom's sister, Aunt Zoey, is overweight,
and so are a bunch of her other relatives.

Funny how my fat gene
comes from Mom.

Dr. Woodn't-You-Like-to-Know
asks if I have a dog.

I nod.
"A fawn pug.
Gigi."

"Tell me about her."

"She's a shelter dog.
I found her trembling

in the back of her cage
when I went to
PugsFurever Rescue's adoption day.
She wouldn't even look at anyone,
as if she figured no one would be good to
   her
because no one ever had been."
I scratch Patches behind his ears,
and he kisses me a thank-you.
"I've been a PugsFurever volunteer ever
   since."

"Why?"

"Dogs are powerless when people
are mean to them.
And lots of people are."

"Hearing you talk about Gigi and
watching you with Patches
tells me you're a kind and
caring person, Ellie."

"Dogs listen when people don't."

She tucks her hair behind her ears.
Wiggles them.
"I'm listening."

I can't help but laugh,
but it's one of those laughs
that turn to tears.

Doc hands me a box of tissues.
I use three before the tears
slow enough so I can talk.

"Mom's on me all the time about my
 weight.
School's a torture chamber,
especially since
my best friend moved away."

"Sounds like you're being bullied.
That hurts. It's scary."

"Nothing I can do about it."

"I can help you confront the bullies
and cope with your feelings,
if you want.
Just say the word."

"The word," I whisper.

Doc used Patches to get me talking.
Doggone good trick.

THE QUESTION

A shark invades my safe harbor.
Enemy Number 3 is at a library study
  carrel,
and when I sit down at one, he gets up
to move a little farther away.

Good!
I didn't want to sit by him, either.
We're even.

One of his shoe soles is loose,
flapping and furling,
and he trips over it.

His eyes scan the room.
Nobody saw it except me.
"What are you staring at,
Megaptera novaeangliae?"

The scientific name for a humpback.
I give him points for originality.

In silence, Enemy Number 3 studies, and
I write in my journal until the bell rings.
"Everyone would leave you alone
if you just lost weight, narwhal,"
he tells me as he gets up to go.
"Have you ever thought about dieting?"

And there it is.

The question everybody asks if you're fat,
as if they're doing you a favor
to suggest it,
as if an overweight person's
never thought about going on a diet.
Oy!

ADJECTIVES AND NOUNS

I remember my first diet.
I was four.
On Thanksgiving,
after I gobbled down turkey and
all the fixings and
reached for one of
Nana's oatmeal raisin cookies,
Mom slapped my hand.
"That does it.
I'm putting you on a diet tomorrow.
You. Are. Fat."

Technically, Mom used *fat*
as an adjective
to describe me,
but with her tone,
she made it a noun
to define me.

Until that moment,
I had never thought about
my body being big
and big being bad,
something to be ashamed of,
to hide,
to hate.

But since then,
I haven't stopped thinking about it.

DIETS, TRIED AND LOST

Thanks to Mom,
if a diet exists,
I've tried it.
Twice.
Probably three times.

Grapefruit diet?
Lost weight and gained
mouth sores
from all the citric acid.

High-fiber diet?
Lost weight and gained
these gross things called hemorrhoids.
You don't want to know.

Chicken diet?
Lost weight and gained
feathers.

Okay. Okay. Okay.
It ended up being
stray feathers from a pillow
stuck to my arm.
But still.

Art Lessons

It's as if all my weight's in my feet,
I drag them so heavily
when I walk in and find
Dr. Woodn't-You-Like-to-Know
at a table topped with art supplies.

"You've *got* to be kidding me."

Art is Viv's thing, not mine.

"We could talk for an hour."
She bats her lashes as she
peers over the reading glasses
that rest on the tip of her nose.

"Art it is, then."
I flash a snarlcasm lip curl:
one part snarl, three parts sarcasm.

She hands me a piece of paper.
"Think of the mean words

105

people have said to you lately.
Pick the one that hurts the most."
She opens a box of colored pencils.
"Have a word in mind?"

I nod.

"Use it in a drawing."

Using gray and metallic silver pencils,
my strokes slowly form a shape, and
some shading pulls your eyes
right to the red.

Dr. Woodn't-You-Like-to-Know
gives my work a sideways glance.
I use my free arm to shield it.
"Eyes on your own work, Doc."

She tries to hide a laugh
and ends up snorting.

Jagged edges form letters,
and I keep going.
I lose track of time
and don't realize
how hard I'm pressing down until
one of the pencils snaps in half.

The doctor cups her hands over mine.

I stop and look down at the paper.
I'm shocked by my drawing.

A fish cut open
with its guts oozing out
and blood spelling *THING*.

BIG OL' FAT THING

I look up at Doc,
who's all quiet and calm.
The drawing didn't freak her out
like it did me.

"All five of us were home, and
we decided to watch a movie.
I was actually enjoying
being with my family for a change.
Then came a beach scene
with a fat girl
spilling out of her bathing suit.
'Look at that big ol' fat thing,'
someone said, and
I pretended not to hear.

"But later, in bed,
I buried my head in my pillow
and cried myself to sleep,

hearing 'Look at that big ol' fat thing'
over and over."

"Who said it?" Doc asks.

I pick up the couch pillow.
Hug it.
Tears sting and well in my eyes,
then run down my cheeks.
"Mom."

Sometimes shock breaks
all the words out of you
like candy from a piñata.

"I think my mom hates me," I begin.
"And I hate thinking that, so
I make myself think about
the times she was nice to me.
Like when I had chicken pox in first
    grade
and Mom curled up in bed with me and
gently scratched my back until I fell
    asleep.
I remember Mom teaching me
how to write haiku.
I remember she gave me

the stuffed rabbit with bunny slippers
that she had as a child.
That was when Nana died
and I couldn't stop crying."

I guess I cling to those moments
like a drowning girl to a life preserver
whenever Mom's words
gut me like a fish.

WHAT I CARRY

If there were a scale in the office,
I'd be tempted to step on it.
I feel twenty pounds lighter.

Sometimes when you're nauseated,
the only way to feel better is to hurl.
And it's as if I've puked up
all the sick feelings
I swallowed that movie night.

"I think you could use a break."
Doc leaves and comes back with water.
"Cheers to you for opening up."
She raises her glass.

"Cheers to you for not gloating."
I tap my glass against hers.

"Pfft," she says, with
a dismissive flick of the wrist.
"I'll do that after you leave."

I say in my best Texas accent,
"Shouldn't you be fixin' to
share some advice?"

"Yep," she tells me. "How about this:
Write down the hurtful words people say
so you don't have to
carry them around in here."
She taps her head
and heart.

SICK AND TIRED

When I don't go for a morning swim,
Dad knows something's up.
He finds me starfishing in bed,
arms and legs stretched out.

"What's going on?"

"I'm sick."
I don't lie.
He touches my forehead.
"No fever."
"Sick and tired of school."
"Anything happen I should know
   about?"
"Just the usual."
"Kinda early in the year for
a mental health day, isn't it?"
"I've been dealing with this
stuff since kindergarten.

113

I'm overdue."
I smown.

He takes off his tie.
"I'll reschedule my clients
and call the school.
Get well fast, though.
Mom comes home from San Antone
t'night."
Dad's Texas twang turns *t'night* to *t'naht*.

"Sure 'nuff."
I tip my pretend cowboy hat.

THE INVITE

"EllieEllieEllie,"
Catalina calls out as I climb
out of the pool,
where I've spent
most of my mental health day.

Her head pops up over the fence.
"Doyoulikefrozencustard?"
She disappears and reappears.
"Momsaysyoucanjoinus."
She disappears and reappears.
"We'releavinginfive."

I jump so she can see me over the fence,
which is hard because of my weight
and even harder without a trampoline.
"I'llgoaskmydad."
I jump up again.
"Berightback."

Catalina cracks up.
"Wegottagetyouatrampoline.
Orspringsinyourshoes.
Orstilts —"

She's still coming up with ideas,
including getting a jet pack,
a few minutes later when I return.
I jump up.
"Hesaysyes."
I don't add,
"BecauseMom'snotaroundtosayno."
I jump up again.
"I'llchangeandberightover."

Watching us,
Dad says
it's probably time
to put a gate in the fence.

JUST AS I AM

I reek of eau de swimming pool chlorine,
my signature perfume,
when we pile in the van.

"Hi, Ellie." Her mom, Sonya, smiles at
  me.
Catalina introduces me to the rest of her
  family.
"Call me Eduardo." Her dad gives a
  mini-wave.
"The big brother, Javier.
Second-oldest, Natalia.
Third-born, Isabella.
And I'm the youngest —
not the baby," Catalina says.

"Same here," I say as
I struggle to squeeze between
the second and third rows of seats.

"I have an idea," Javier says.
I tense up, waiting for the joke.
"You two sit here."
He pats on the second-row seat.
"Nat, Izzy, and I will take the back."
"Good idea," Sonya says.
"Guests should always have the best."

They accepted me,
just as I am,
in five seconds flat.
Why can't my family do that?

FOOD CHAIN

At the custard place,
an overweight woman
eyes me from head to toe,
and puckers her lips in disgust
as if she's bitten into
a sour lemon.

It doesn't make sense
for another fat person to judge me,
but a Fat Girl Rule
gives her the power:
The fatter you are,
the lower you are
on the food chain.

Then she looks over at Javier
and grips her purse.
I don't want her insulting
Catalina's family,

so I say,
"I only eat purses when I'm hangry."

"This custard's the best, isn't it?"
Catalina asks me, ignoring the lady.

"Looks like she loves it
a little too much," the rude woman says.
"She needs to lose weight."

"And you need to gain manners!"
Catalina hooks her arm around mine
and whisks me away.

ALIEN ENCOUNTER

Fat people have one superpower.
Their eyes are rulers, measuring spaces
to see if they'll fit.
I activate mine when
Catalina's family picks out a pink picnic
  table.
I'll fit, but it'll be tight.
I suck my stomach in as we sit.

Catalina scoots close to me
and whispers,
"Does that rude lady think I'm . . .
an alien?"

Huh? I give Catalina a blank look.

"Earth to Ellie.
Does she think I'm an alien?
You know. Like an illegal?"

"An illegal alien?"

"Duh?" She gives me a Spock salute.
"What did you think I meant, a Vulcan?"

We laugh so hard my belly jiggles,
drawing extra attention to it.
I break a Fat Girl Rule in public,
and I don't care.
I want to laugh with my friend.

Then Catalina turns serious.
"Lots of people look at us
like that lady looked at Javier.
I mean, we're Mexican Americans in Texas.
We're *the* stereotype of illegals."

"Stereotypes stink.
They give people an excuse to
hate people who are different
instead of taking the time
to get to know them."

"Nicely said.
It's almost like you're a writer or
  something."
She playfully elbows me.

Then Catalina hangs down her head.
"I hate the way people look at us
and how they treat us."

Does everybody
make somebody
feel like a nobody?

SHATTERING STEREOTYPES

There's a Fat Girl Rule
I'm going to have to rethink:
When eating out,
never finish first.

That's a rule because
usually people expect you to wolf down
 food
as if you're out of control.
But I eat my ice cream so slowly,
I end up sipping custard soup.

I also eat slowly because
I keep thinking about stereotypes.
People stereotype me
all the time, too.

They think fat people are dumb.
I'm at the top of my class.

They think we're slobs.
My room is spotless.

They think we're unhappy.

That's true.

But they think I'm unhappy
because I'm fat.
The truth is,
I'm unhappy because
they bully me
about being fat.

Let it Rip

This is what you'll find in the dictionary
when you look up the definition of gym:

> **gym (noun) \ˈjim**
> : school-approved body-shaming
> session.

Well, that's what it should say.

Athletes love PE, an easy A.
Everyone else just tries to survive it.
If you don't have hang-ups about your
  body
before you take phys ed, you will after.
You're literally graded on
what it can and cannot do.

Like a pack of feral cats
with a trapped mouse,
the other team tortures me slowly

during dodgeball by
making me the last one standing.
Then the players pounce,
zinging me with all the balls at once,
leaving stinging welts.
Outside and in.

Afterward, I change in a bathroom stall
instead of the locker room.
But my clothes aren't hanging
on the hook where I left them.

Laughter bounces off
the cement-block walls.
I don't have butterflies in my stomach.
I have pterodactyls.

Fat Girl Rule:
When you hear laughter,
someone's laughing at you.

Still in my gym uniform,
I square my shoulders and
slam open the stall door.
I find Marissa trying on my
new orange peasant top.

"Hey, Kortnee," Marissa yells,
"two people can probably fit
in Splash's shirt! Try it on with me."
"No way," Kortnee yells back.
"Not getting fat girl cooties all over me!"

When I hear a seam rip, something rips
    in me.
I turn into a feral cat cornering two mice.
"Enough, Ski Slope Nose
and Moon Crater Face!"

Each girl freezes — like an armadillo in
    headlights
under my glare.

I snatch my shirt out of Marissa's hands.
"Got something to say about my body
when you have obvious flaws, too?"

"We were just joking.
Lighten up," Marissa tells me.
They silently slip on their clothes,
and I go back to the stall to dress.
I won't raise my hand in any classes today
so no one will see the rip
in the armhole.

Standing up for myself
is a good thing, right?
So why do I feel
so mean,
so sad?

SIBLING BRIBERY

Forget sibling rivalry.
I'm all about sibling bribery.

Mom, Dad, and Anaïs are busy,
so Liam's supposed to drive me home,
but he offers me twenty bucks
to take a DART bus instead.
I take it and make him give me
cash for the fare, too.

Liam's taking some girl to the mall.
I get it — who wants their kid sister
    tagging along?
But I'm not supposed to use
public transportation until I'm thirteen.
That's a little over a year away,
so I'll be fine.

With an app,
I figure out which bus I need.

But as soon as I sit down,
I realize I've made a mistake.
Two teenagers start in on me.
"Please, I beg of you,
kill me if I ever look like that."
"Oh, trust me, I would."

An old woman pats my hand.
I think she's trying to comfort me
until she says, "Chubby, aren't you?"
  and
pinches the fat on my left arm.

"Ouch!" I say, jerking back.

I bolt up to get off
at the next stop.

As others get off the bus
and some try to get on,
I become a pinball,
bounced and sent flying
into someone,
then someone else,
over and over.

Finally, the crowd parts,
and I'm off the awful bus.

131

I take a deep breath,
thinking I've finally caught a break.
Then I smell it,
that earthy scent of
the first raindrops of a storm.
I can't run fast enough to escape, and
I don't know where to go anyway.
So I close my eyes and
let the rain wash over me.
Until lightning crackles.

"Hurry!" An arm taps my shoulder.
"This way!"
It's Catalina.
My friend.

Texas Twister

"I thought I'd have to swim home."
I wipe my face as if it's just wet from rain,
not tears, after we climb into Javier's car,
full of Catalina's sisters.

"Good thing Catalina spotted you.
It's a wicked storm.
I'm going to pull over.
I can barely see."
Javier parks at a convenience store.

"There's a song for every occasion,"
Catalina says, and blares
"En la tormenta" by Días Divertidos
from her phone.

The five of us bebop to the beat,
rocking the car —
until we hear the tornado siren.

"Let's make a run for the store!" Javier
  shouts,
and we dash through the rain.

Inside, we hear the news.
A tornado hit the next town —
and it's spinning straight toward us.

BUSTED

I'm not a Goody Two-shoes
or a tattletale by choice.
It's just that I can never get away with
breaking any kind of rule.
I always get caught.

Dad texts,
Where are you and Liam?
Are you okay?
It's terrible out!

I'm busted.
I text back,
Liam went to mall,
paid me to take a DART bus.
I got off at wrong stop.
I don't lie.
Safe now with Catalina.

Taking shelter at a store.
Explain more later.

YES, YOU WILL!
All caps.
Crap.

The tornado turns into
a funnel cloud and fades away.
When we get the all clear,
I quickly stock up on snacks
for my secret stash.

I'm going to need them.

I may never see the light of day again.

FIX MOM'S THINKING

If only you could exchange siblings
like you can horrible gifts.
I'd trade Liam for Javier in a heartbeat.

When I thank him for the ride home,
he smiles and says, "No problem, kiddo.
Glad you didn't have to swim home after all."

"Wanna do homework together?"
Catalina asks.
"I wish! But I can't today.
Doctor's appointment."
Catalina tucks her head into her shirt,
like a turtle into its shell —
a makeshift mask from germs.
"You sick?"
"Not that kind of doctor.
A therapist."
It slips out.

"What?"

She unturtles.

"Mom thinks something's wrong with me since I'm as big as a whale."

"Well, that is messed up."

"Gee, thanks."

"No! Your mom's thinking. Not you!"

Could Catalina be right?
Could it be Mom's thinking that needs
  fixing
and
not me?

Missing Viv

Survived a storm,
thanks to Catalina,
but may not survive my punishment
for riding a DART bus.

"Hey, no texting while I'm talking,"
Dad says as he drives me to see Doc.
"But Viv heard about the tornado
and wanted to know if we're okay.
I had to tell her what happened."
Just then my phone pings
and my dad sighs.

Why were you riding that bus?
With Catalina?
I'm jealous.
You still love me best?
Text yes or no.
LOL.

I start to reply, but Dad interrupts.
"That's enough."

"But, Dad —"
"No buts.
I want to know what in the Sam Hill
made you think it was okay
to ride the bus by yourself?"

"I had no other way to get home," I tell
    him.
"Where was Liam?" he asks.
"Liam had a date."

"Well now,
this story has more twists than
a pretzel factory."
Dad shakes his head as
he drums his fingers
on the steering wheel.

"Liam will be in a mess of trouble.
You can hang your hat on that.
But you're a smart girl, Ellie.
You could have called me or
your aunt Zoey.
I expect you to make a better decision,

one that will keep you safe,
if something like this ever happens again.
You hear?"

I nod and cry.

Dad thinks my tears won't stop
because of what Liam did.
Who cares about him?
I'm crying because I didn't
get to reply to Viv's text.
I'm crying because she's so far away.
I'm crying because
I'm missing Viv so much.

LET THERE BE
LIGHT — SABERS

What's more frightening
than a twister coming at you
is a tornado of emotions inside of you.

I want to talk to Viv, not a therapist.
I flop down on the couch.

"What's going on?" Doc asks.
I fold my arms across my chest.

"Oh, we're back to that again.
Got it.
If you need anything,
I'll just be over there
practicing my Jedi training."

She walks over to the shelves
stocked with games and art supplies,
grabs a lightsaber, and
turns it on.

142

Pshewww.
She spins and slices it through the air
in some kind of imaginary duel.
She grabs another saber
and throws it to me.
"Help me, Obi-El!"

Oh, what the heck.
Pshewww.
I join the battle.

Every time I strike Doc's saber,
she defends herself.

"So, tell me about school."
"Marissa and Kortnee —"
"Oh, yes, the dark side," she chimes in.
"Marissa put on my new shirt after gym.
Told Kortnee they'd probably both fit in it.
And ripped it."

I lunge, strike a low blow.
Doc steps up onto a chair to escape.

I swing,
she defends,
and we lock sabers,
form an X.

143

"Did you attack back?"
"I made fun of Marissa's nose and
Kortnee's acne."
Doc steps closer.
The sabers hum and buzz,
glow red and blue.
"Did that feel good?"

"Actually, no."

She turns off her saber.
"Let's start with that."

I flop back down on the couch.
"When I tried to stand up for myself,
why did I end up feeling worse than
when they bully me?"

"Think about our little duel.
What did you learn?"

"That you like toys?"
"True, but focus on the battle.
Did I ever use my saber to strike you?"

I shake my head.
"So I can defend myself
without attacking others?"
"Good Jedi, you are."

Technology Tricks

When grown-ups fully understand
  technology,
kids will be in big trouble.
Until then, we rule the planet.
To punish me,
Dad took my phone so I can't text,
but I have a computer and
I can email texts to Viv.

I'm grounded.
No phone for now.
That's why I didn't answer.
No reason
to be jealous of Catalina.
You and I are besties.
Will always be.
I hate that you're a thousand miles
  away.

She replies,
Feels like a million.
So tell me about
this storm and bus thing.

I tell her everything that happened,
and ask,
So how was your day?

She replies,
Equally horrible.
The divorce is final.
I'm officially without a family.

If only I could text a hug.

CHOOSING SIDES

Sometimes I fear Splitsville
for my parents, too.
I try to picture what life would be like
spending part of my week with Dad,
the other part with Mom.
Half of my stuff at one house,
the rest at another.
Constantly packing and unpacking.
Never feeling settled.
No one place to call home.

But would I feel relieved, too?
No more hearing
them fighting because of
me
would be nice.

147

Of course, if I had to choose
which parent to live with,
I know it'd be Dad,
not because I love him more,
but because I'm not sure
Mom loves me at all.

WHERE HATE COMES FROM

Will there ever be world peace
when families can't even agree
on what to have for dinner?

Dad wants barbecue.
Mom wants the latest, greatest trendy
  restaurant.
Anaïs wants all things non-American.
Liam wants pizza.
It doesn't matter what I want.
Wherever we go,
I don't even bother to look at the menu.
Mom always decides what I get.

We go to Mom's choice,
and while we wait for our food,
a little boy from the next table comes over.
Dad plays up his accent.
"Well, howdy, little fella."

The boy looks at me and then at his dad,
who nods and grins.
The boy faces me again.
"You're fat."
He runs toward his dad,
stops, comes back, and adds,
"Oh, and save some food
for the rest of us, would ya?"

The little boy gets
a high five from his dad,
and everyone at their table dies laughing.

In a flash, my dad's at their table.
The little boy's dad stands up.
Dad towers over the guy.
Now I can imagine
what Dad looked like
growing up on the Panhandle ranch
and wrangling bucking bulls.

A hush falls over the restaurant.
"You. Owe. My. Daughter. An. Apology."
"I'm sorry she's fat?" The boy's dad
    chuckles.

The manager comes over,
steps between them.
"Let's all remain calm."

Mom stands up.
"Stop, Phillip. Let's go.
We've been humiliated enough."

We?!

"We are out of here."
Mom tugs on Dad's arms as
she tells us kids to go to the car.

Like I said,
Mom always decides what I get.

A COMET'S TALE

I've been keeping a secret,
Viv texts.

You're scaring me.
Are you okay?

See for yourself.
She sends me a link to a video.
A mascot that looks like a snowball,
but with a blue-and-orange flame tail,
dances onto a football field.
The crowd yells,
"Go, Comet, go!"
The band's drums pound:
pum, pum-pum, pum.
Comet wags the tail
at the opposing team:
whoosh, whoosh-whoosh, whoosh.

The home team erupts in
cheers.

Comet dances until
the football players run onto the
 field,
its arms morphing into snakes
and hips making figure eights.

I recognize those moves!
Viv is the mascot!

Then Viv and I video-chat, and
it's so good to hear my friend's voice.
"I've never been cheered on
by my classmates before.
Being chosen as the mascot
is a huge honor."

"I'm so proud of you!
So happy for you!"
I mean it.
But I'm also envious.

Viv's found a cool way
to be okay

with her size.
How do I do that?
To me,
that seems as impossible as
finding a unicorn.

LIAM'S WISH

In English class, my teacher says
that even the worst villain
has a bit of good inside.

She obviously hasn't met my brother.

I find an extra notebook in my backpack
that Mom must have thought was mine
when she was straightening up.
I flip it open.
It's Liam's writing journal.

Having a fat sister stinks.
We can't do stuff
like go to amusement parks
'cause she can't fit on the rides.

And when we go out,
people stare at all of us,
not just her.

Sometimes it ticks me off,
and I want to punch people.
Mostly I just wish I didn't have
to be seen with her.

Liam is so full of hate for me,
I can't even think of him
as my brother anymore.
DNA doesn't make you family.
Love does.
Actions do.

Outside, in a rage,
I tear page after page
out of his journal,
toss them into the hungry mouth
of the chiminea,
and light a fire.

As flames
devour his words and
smoke swirls up my nose,
I realize the anger I feel right now
isn't just about Liam's
horrible, heartbreaking words in the
   journal.

It's from all the words I've ever wanted
to say back to him.
Words that've been
smoldering inside of me.

It's time to let them go.
They don't seem to bother him one bit,
   but
they're hurting me.

WORSE THAN PEE ON CARPET

"Eliana Elizabeth Montgomery-
    Hofstein!
What do you think you're doing?!"
Mom screams as I use
the garden hose to extinguish
the last flames.

"Your dad's office!"
She points as if I don't know the way.
"Now!"

She follows me.
"Phillip, do you know what
your daughter did?"
her voice calls ahead,
warning him that we're about to storm
    the door.
Once in Dad's office,
Mom points to the couch.

"Sit!"
My dog and I instantly obey.

Gigi looks up at me
with her bulging pug eyes like,
This is worse than
pee-on-the-new-white-carpet bad, right?
I nod.

The secret to surviving childhood
so far has been knowing when
to keep my mouth shut.
But I am *not* a child anymore.
I have feelings.
I have thoughts.
I have the right to express them both.

Mom fills Dad in and
starts in on me again.
"You know the rules.
No. Starting. Fires. Alone.
Ever! Ever!! Ever!!!"

"What did you burn?" Dad asks.

"Just some nasty writing
I didn't want anyone else to read."
I don't lie.

159

"So tearing it into pieces and
tossing it into the trash wasn't an
    option?"
Mom throws her hands up in the air.

"Nope! Not when you're always
going through my trash."

I can't believe I just said
these words aloud.

And it's so worth it to see
the shocked look on her face.

"You should hear all the words
I want to say to you, Mom."

I may be grounded,
but I'm lighter than a balloon
as I float to my room.

SHABBAT

In the Lone Star State,
Friday nights in the fall
are all about football,
but not at our house,
although we could use
a few referees
— especially after this week,
when it's been
one scrimmage after another.

We gather in the dining room.
I dread when we greet each other
with hugs and "Shabbat shalom."
I prefer cuddling with a porcupine
over hugging Liam.

I look forward to the blessing, though.
Even though Mom's a Christian,
she participates.

My parents place their
hands on my head
and pray over me.
I always focus on Mom's voice.
"May God show you favor
and be gracious to you.
May God show you kindness
and grant you peace."

Favor.
Kindness.
Peace.
Yes, I'd like that.

From Mom.
For a change.

WHALING SEASON

Mrs. Boardman, my English teacher,
wants us to read all kinds of books,
not just our favorite genres or authors.
"Reading should be like
dining at a buffet," she says.
"You have a lot to choose from:
fiction, poetry, graphic novels, and more.
There are books galore!
Eat them all up!"
After we read,
we're supposed to write about
the books in our journals.
A teacher who talks about
books, food, and writing?
Trifecta.

"I know which book I'm reading,"
I tell Mrs. Boardman after class.

"*Song for a Whale.*
It's about a whale whose song
can't be heard by those around him."

I know what it's like
not to be heard.

Unfortunately, Marissa overhears me.
"It figures you'd want to read about
a big old whale."
Her eyes shoot a harpoon, and
she claps for herself five times.
She claps whenever she completes a task.
Always five short, rapid claps.

Her habit must be quite awkward
in the bathroom.

"Whales are
unique,
beautiful,
and powerful," Mrs. Boardman says.
"If you bothered to learn more about
   them,
you'd know that."

I give five quick claps.

COMFORTER

Mrs. Boardman asks me to stay after class.
"Your last assignment."
She hands me back the poem I wrote.
"It's wonderful.
I'd love to hear you read it."

"Memories wrap around me
when I'm wrapped up in my quilt.
Memories of watching Bobeshi
weave squares cut from old clothes
into a celebration of Hofstein ancestry.

"Each tells a tale.
Baby pajamas.
Lace and satin wedding gown.
Striped cotton jacket with a gold star.

"My hands glide over the faded fabric
worn velvety smooth over the years.

Years of hiding under it after school and
  then
when muffling my cries after Bobeshi
  moved away.

"Memories warm me more than the fabric
as I snuggle beneath it,
feeling Bobeshi's love living on
as the quilt,
holding and comforting me."

Mrs. Boardman finger-snaps.
"Your first reading.
You're officially a poet."

BREAK AWAY

School break.
Two words that spark
joy
in the hearts of students everywhere.

Family trip.
Two words that spark
fights
in the car, the plane, the hotel —
  everywhere.

Dad booked a fall foliage tour.
Two flights and countless hours
just to see dying leaves
in New Hampshire and Vermont.
I'll never understand grown-ups.

And then he throws in a surprise.
To tick an item off his bucket list,

we're going to Niagara Falls, too.
A long road trip.

To top it off,
there's no pool.
Even if there were,
I'd just as soon
tie bloody fish around my waist
and dive into an ocean of sharks
than swim with strangers.

SAY CHEESE

The universe should warn you
when something horrible
is about to happen,
give you a chance to
take a deep breath
before your breath
gets taken away.

While my family fights over
what to do next,
I watch the water thunder over
Horseshoe Falls in New York.

Someone taps me on the shoulder.
A girl speaking a language
I've never heard points
to her camera and me.
I nod and reach for the camera

169

to take a picture of
her with her friends.

But faster than the flowing water,
the giggling group surrounds me
as the girl
takes our picture.

And I'm in the center of it.
I imagine the social media post:
"Girls Encounter Fatzilla in America."
It goes viral.
I'm a global joke.

What do I do?

I think about what Doc said.
I have the right
to stand up for myself,
to defend myself.

I force myself to
walk over to them and
use my hands to say
I'm willing to take their picture.

I snap a group photo and
then one of the falls before

turning my back on them for
just a second,
just long enough.
Then I give back the camera.

When the girls walk away,
I toss the camera's memory card
over the falls.

HARD TO TALK ABOUT

For the first time,
I'm really glad I have
an appointment with Doc.
As soon as I sit down,
I show her
the latest ugly word I wrote
on the ever-growing list of
hurtful things people say to me.

> **mon · ster** (noun) \\´män(t)-st´r\\
> 1 : a human grotesquely deviating
> from the normal shape.
> 2 : one who inspires horror or
> disgust.
> 3 : me.

I create Niagara Falls in Texas when
Doc asks me to tell her what happened
   and,

before I can get one word out,
the tears flow.

I cry so hard,
so long,
Dad hears me.

Then I hear Dad
pacing in the waiting room.
A few times his cowboy boots stop
right at the door and
the handle starts to turn and
stops and
turns again, until finally
I open the door and
let him in, and
he sits and holds me
like I'm a little girl and
rocks me until
I'm all cried out.

More Time

Sometimes
you just need
more time.

Our session is over,
but Doc says we need to talk.
So Dad goes back to the waiting room,
never knowing what made me so upset.
I don't know if
I'll ever tell him.
I don't want to ruin
his good memories of Niagara Falls.

"I feel so stupid,
not figuring out what they were up to.
And I feel so guilty for what I did.
I stole something.
I've never done that before.
I destroyed their vacation photos."

"You feel guilty because
you're a good person who
made a bad decision to
snatch the card rather than
defend yourself."
Doc hands me
a piece of stationery and a pen.
"Write that girl a letter
and confront her."

DEAR STRANGER

Dear girl who tapped me on the shoulder:

What made you think
it was okay
to take a photo of me
without my permission
just because I don't look like you?

What if someone
took photos of you,
showing everyone
what makes you different?
What part of you
would you want to hide?

Do you think it's funny
to make another person feel
like less of a human?

PS
You must feel
kind of bad
about yourself
if you feel good
when you hurt someone else.

PPS
Sorry I stole the memory card.
That was wrong of me,
no matter what you did.

TAKING A STAND

It's been a quiet week at school,
so I should have known something
was coming.
On Friday, when I go to my locker
before heading to the library,
I find a picture taped to it.
It's my head —
photoshopped on a whale's body.

I tear it down, ball it up, and
throw it at Marissa.
Hard.
Wham!
I'd aimed for her head,
but hit her heart.
Well, where her heart would be,
if she had one.
She just snickers and walks away.

And then, as if that weren't enough,
Enemy Number 3 decides
to start his old lunchtime routine
of slamming his back against the hallway
  wall
as if I take up all the room.
"Get back! Make room! Thar she blows!"

But instead of lowering my head in shame,
I hold my head up high and
lock eyes with Enemy Number 3 until
I'm standing in front of him.

"You think you're funny," I tell him.
"But you're just plain old mean.
Maybe I can't stop you,
but I can at least
make you look me in the eye
every time you do it.
And I will, from now on."

As I walk away,
I realize I've been
starfishing —
starting to claim my right
to take up space
in this place.

MAKING A DIFFERENCE

Doc wouldn't approve of
me throwing stuff at Marissa.
Oops.
But I think she'd give me
a giant thumbs-up for
how I confronted Enemy Number 3.
I'm not the best at math,
but even I know that
one out of two isn't bad.

Then I notice Mrs. Boardman
is in the hallway, too.
"Come with me to my classroom
for a minute, Ellie,"
she says.

Mrs. Boardman motions for me
to have a seat.
I flop down at a desk,

and we both stare at
my shaking hands.

"Confrontations aren't easy," she says.
"I'm sorry some students
make school hard for you.
I know it takes lots of
strength to face them.
I think you're brave.
You're a great writer and have a
way with words.
I hope you'll keep using your voice
to share your point of view.
To show others what it's like
to walk in your shoes.
And maybe they'll feel empowered to
stand up to their bullies."

Her words make me feel better.
Today I faced my bullies.
And maybe I can show other kids
that it can be done.

PERMANENTLY ALTERED

I think Mom's changing when she rips
the latest weight-loss articles off the
  fridge,
but then I see she's only making room
for bariatric surgery success stories.
Ugh.

I guess it doesn't matter
that her sister, my aunt Zoey,
almost died from bariatric surgery.
Or that I'm only eleven, almost twelve.
According to most doctors,
you need to be at *least* fourteen
to have weight-loss surgery.

But if Mom wants me to have it,
she'll find a way.
I realize that today,
with the articles she found

about a twelve-year-old who had it,
and — oh my gosh —
even a five-year-old.
And
a
two-year-old!

Five years old.
Two.
Their bodies cut open and
permanently, surgically altered.
Just because they're fat.

My aunt,
despite the risks,
decided to have the surgery.
Just about everything
that could go wrong did.
I still remember sitting by her bed,
holding her cold hands,
and listening to a machine breathe for her.
She survived, after six weeks in the ICU.

How could Mom
risk putting me through
all of that?

SWARMED

Sharks usually attack when
a whale is alone or distressed.

The sharks at school
swarm around me
the day I break a desk in math class.

First the desk legs steadily, slowly spread
   out,
like the legs on a cartoon horse
after a fat cowboy saddles up for a ride.

I struggle to escape,
but I'm stuck.
With a final creak of the bending metal
and crack of the wood,
the desk and I crumble to the floor.

I am a sea turtle on its back,
trying to get out of the rubble,

trying to get up,
trying to will the earth to open up
and swallow me whole.

The sharks circle.
Sink their teeth in.
Take turns biting
with laughter and words.

"Splash broke a chair!"

"Duuuuuuude! That was metal!"

"Collapsed like a soda can."

"Poor desk didn't stand a chance."

Metal and wood cut into and jab
my stomach, sides, back, and legs.
It hurts to breathe.
"Help me.
Somebody.
Please."

They just keep laughing.

SCREWED

It's like Moses with the Red Sea as
Mr. Harrington parts the crowd.
"What is going on in here?!"
My math teacher sees me,
frees me,
and stretches his hands toward mine.
"And none of you were kind enough to
    help!"
"As if one person could help her up,"
says someone.
"As if one fire department could,"
says another.

Mr. Harrington makes big circles
over his head,
like a cowboy winding up a lasso.
"Detention for all of you."
Everyone groans.

186

He examines the desk,
says a bad word under his breath.
"Who took the bolts off the screws?
More detention for all y'all if
the person who did it doesn't start
    talkin'."

Kortnee raises her hand.
"Guilty."

Math question:
What's the probability of Marissa
not being the one to tell Kortnee to
    do it?

A Round of Applause

My jaws clench so tight
I think my teeth will crumble
in my mouth like damp chalk.

Marissa laughs,
mouths, "Blubberbelly."

I lunge forward.
Mr. Harrington steps in front of me.
"Walk away, Ellie."

His voice booms again,
"Kortnee, principal's office!"

A few people clap as
she struts down the aisle
and out the door.
"Best prank ev-ah."

"No more comments!"
Mr. Harrington eyes the room.
"Let's make that two days of detention.
Wanna make it three? Keep talkin'."

Silence.
Does that mean they agree or
they're afraid to defend me or
they just don't want more detention?
I'll never know.

"I'm disappointed in all of you," he says.
"Even if you didn't
remove the chair bolts,
you knew someone did,
so you're just as responsible
for what happened.
You should have spoken up.
History books are full
of horrible things happening
because people sit back
and do and say nothing.
To you,
what happened today's okay

because it wasn't you
being bullied.
But one day,
it could be.
Remember that."

No Ignoring it

My eyes zoom in on a picture frame
on the math teacher's desk.

There's a photo of Mr. Harrington,
his wife, and their little daughter,
who's not so little,
eating watermelon and
celebrating the Fourth of July.
His daughter smashes her
whole face into the red flesh of the fruit,
juice dripping from her chin,
stray seeds sticking to her chubby cheeks.
So that's why he stood up for me.

Mr. Harrington motions for me
to join him in the hallway.
"Call someone to pick you up.
Go home and have a good cry.
When you come back on Monday,

pretend like this never happened.
Just ignore them."

"Mr. Harrington, you're a math teacher.
What's the probability of that
changing anything?"

I start to walk away, but turn back.
"And I hope you never tell your daughter
to just have a good cry and
ignore bullies.
She deserves better."

"You're right, Ellie,"
Mr. Harrington calls out after me.
"She does deserve better.
And so do you.
Maybe better advice might be to
spend your energy focusing on
what and who makes
you happy,
instead of focusing on the fools
who don't like you
— for whatever reason."

BRACE, BRACE, BRACE

Me: Today can't get any worse.
Universe: Challenge accepted.

When I sit down to dinner,
Liam starts in as he smears butter on an
    ear of corn.
"Splash broke a chair in math class
    today."

Of course he knows about my
    humiliation —
he's friends with Marissa's brother.

Like a passenger on a nose-diving plane,
I brace for impact.

But then I decide to speak up.
I do know my worth.
"It wasn't like that, Liam, and you
    know it."

"Were you" —
one row of corn gone, lips smacking —
"or were you not" —
second row gone, lips smacking —
"on the floor in math class?"
Third row gone, lips smacking.

"You know I was set up!" I shout.

"Can't we send her off to some fat camp,
or make her have surgery or something?"
Now Liam's talking with his mouth full,
spraying corn bits across the table.

"I'm sure you wish
I'd never been born.
Well, guess what?
I wish that about you!"

"Ellie —"
Mom doesn't finish her sentence.
Inside my head, I finish it for her:
You big ol' fat thing!

Anaïs looks at me with sad puppy eyes.
Pity.
Perfect.

"Stop it!"
Dad bangs his tea glass down on the
  table
like a judge with a gavel
calling for order in the court.
His hands form
here's-the-church-and-here's-the-steeple.
He gives me all of his attention.
Sometimes I can't tell if that's a dad
  thing
or one of his psychiatrist moves.
"What happened?"

Just like a writer,
I tell the story
of what Marissa and Kortnee did
— except I realize the story
doesn't have an end.
Not yet.

No Love

Like Texas tea
gushing from an oil rig,
Dad erupts.
"The school has got
to put a stop
to this bullying!

"Dinner is over!" he says, and
starts clearing the table,
slamming the plates as he stacks them.
Mom starts gathering leftovers to take
into the kitchen.

Liam tries to swipe another lamb chop.
"Hey, I'm still eating here."
"Go. To. Your. Room," Mom orders.

Only I stay seated —
but nobody pays any attention
to me.

With the swing door propped open
from the dining room to the kitchen,
I have a front-row seat for all the action.

It's like a tennis match
when my parents lob words as they argue,
except there's no love.

"I'm calling the school."

"You're just going to make it worse,"
  Mom says.
I silently side with her on this one.

"There are laws."
Dad scrapes the food off the plates.

"Not easily enforceable."
Mom loads the dishwasher.

Crash!

"Oh no, Phillip! You ruined a plate!"
Mom sounds more upset by the broken
  dish
than by what's happening to me.

"Marissa and Kortnee have to be punished.
Nobody deserves to be treated like this!"

Dad grabs the broom.
As he sweeps up the pieces,
Mom bends down with the dustpan and
  says,
"It'll get worse if we make a big deal
  about it.
If she lost weight,
all of this would stop."

"You're incredible, Miriam.
You know that?"

"And you're ignoring the effect
her weight has on everything."

"Miriam, someone hurt our child.
Don't you get that?"

"What you don't get, Phillip —"

I've heard enough.
I get up, and
they don't even notice when I leave.

Checking on Me

Lap after lap,
I slap, slap, slap
my arms against the water
and kick my legs fast and hard.

Then I dive under
to yell the words I wish I'd said
at school and during dinner.

Spent, I exhale through my nose,
creating a trail of bubbles to the top,
where I find Catalina
sitting near the steps.

"Never heard you splash so hard, so long.
Thought maybe something was wrong.
Came through the new gate to check on
  you."
She squints.
"Your eyes are really red."

"Chlorine," I mumble.

"Friends shouldn't lie to friends.
What's wrong?"

I shake my head.
"I just can't —"

I dive under,
swimming and screaming
until my lungs burn for air.
When I surface, Catalina's still there.

She's sitting on the edge, closer to me.
I glide over to Catalina.
"Thank you," I say,
my voice hoarse
from all the crying.

"I don't know what happened to you
or why people are so mean, Ellie,
but I do know
whatever someone did is
a reflection of them.
Not you."

FROM *I* TO *WE*

The next day,
I go for a swim,
like always.
And Catalina sits on the deck
practicing her guitar,
like always.

I finish my laps
and tread water
at the side of the pool.
"I don't think
you should stay there."

She stops strumming.
"Do you want some privacy?"

"I want some company."

She sets down the guitar and
yanks off her jeans and T-shirt.

She's in her swimsuit.
"I've worn it
under my clothes for weeks.
I thought you'd never ask."

We swim.
We.
You can pack a powerful punch
in a two-letter word.

Catalina and I circle,
splash,
dive,
and surface,
just like the documentary
I once saw showing a humpback
and a dolphin,
an unlikely pair,
playing in the water.

We're mismatched
in all kinds of ways,
yet we found each other
in the ocean of
people on the planet
and became friends.

TREAT ME BETTER

When Anaïs stands in my doorway,
I know something's up.
"What do you want?"

She sits beside me on my bed.
"To talk.
To tell you I'm so sorry
about the whole chair thing."

"Why do you care?"

Anaïs scrunches up her face.
"What's that supposed to mean?"

"You never defend me when
Mom or Liam insults me."

She hangs her head down.
"I should."

The silence in the room's heavy,
like the air when one storm's passed
but another's on the horizon.

"I haven't been the best sister," Anaïs
  admits.
"Or even a good one, for that matter."

I sit silently.
Don't disagree.

"Okay, I suck as a sister,"
she finally blurts out.
"But I haven't treated you
as badly as Liam has."

"Oh, well then, that changes everything.
I'll go ahead and order
your Sister of the Year Award.
I'll let you know when it arrives.
Feel free to hold your breath until then."

I point to the door.
"Out! I have homework to do."

Anaïs gives me a sad smile.
"You're pretty funny, and I know
I'm lucky you're my sister."

She puts her hand on my shoulder,
and I pull away.
"I'm sorry."

"Saying you're sorry
doesn't undo all you've done."

"You're right, you're right.
All I can do is
treat you better starting now.
And I promise I will."

Sisters at Last

I can't help it.
I want Anaïs to feel
some of the hurt
that I feel.
So I let her have it.

"Do you even realize you haven't
called me by my real name
since my fifth birthday?"

Tears well in her eyes.
"Don't you dare cry, Anaïs!
You don't have a right to cry!
You're the reason
everyone calls me Splash!"

But she can't help it.
She buries her face in her hands
and sobs.

Maybe
it's from watching Anaïs cry.
Maybe
it's from just thinking about
all the years of being called Splash.
But a wave of sadness hits.

I surrender to the sadness.
It's so
heavy,
dark,
and cold,
it takes my breath away.

Anaïs leans in and whispers,
"I do care.
I want to be here for you."

I let her wrap her arms around me,
draw me close,
hold me tight,
tighter,
while today's dammed tears break free
and we both
can't stop sobbing.

CALLED BY NAME

An oyster can turn
something irritating into
a rare and beautiful pearl.
People can do that, too.

Anaïs and I end up talking for hours.
It's as if we're making up for lost time.

She says seeing my bruises
after the prank with the chair
woke her up.
"I just kept thinking,
'I can't believe they hurt Ellie.
I mean, they really hurt her.'"

I don't tell her the bruises
hurt less than
the words they've said,
that there are wounds she can't see.

I don't say anything
because
I can only focus on one thing.

She called me Ellie.

IGNORED OUT OF EXISTENCE

Surprise, surprise.
Dad calling the school
about the chair incident
doesn't stop Marissa and Kortnee from
being mean to me.

Now,
instead of torturing me,
they ignore me —
and have their friends
ignore me, too.

At first I think
being ignored is better
than being humiliated.
But then I wonder.

Because when people look right through
  you,
it's like you don't even matter.
Like you don't exist.
And everyone is fine
with that.

DIFFERENT AND OKAY

For history class,
we're supposed to write a report about
a way in which society's changed
over the years.
I'm writing about
how the world's view of
beauty based on size has changed.

With the help of our librarian, Mrs. Pochon,
I find reliable sources on the internet and
books of photos of paintings and sculptures
from a hundred to a thousand years ago.
They're from cultures around the world
and show girls with
rolls and curves.

Girls like me.

I learn big girls,
even obese ones,

were once seen as
normal,
preferred,
beautiful.

I can't imagine a world so . . .
safe.

As I flip through the pages,
I start thinking that if I'd lived back
    then,
it could have been me
in the pictures,
as sculptures,
as art.

My body seen as
pretty.

Mrs. Pochon comes and
checks to see how I'm doing.
"Finding everything okay?"
"I'm finding a lot,
and it's fascinating."

"Yes," she says.
"Ideas of beauty change with time.
Who knows what people will think

years from now about
what we consider beautiful today."

After she leaves, I think about this.
It would be great if people realized that
we're all different, in all kinds of ways,
and different is okay.

But I bet there will always be some
who don't get it.
What's important is that
I do.

SPEWING ANGER

When it comes to Doc,
I'm learning to expect the unexpected.
Today she's dressed like the White Rabbit
for Halloween.

"Do you celebrate?" she asks.

"Not so much.
Mom's not a fan because
of all that candy.
I'm not a fan because
costumes never fit.
It's truly a night of horror."

Doc nods and we both laugh when
her rabbit ears fall off.

When I fork over my list of ugly words,
Doc flips through them and stops.
"Tell me about this one: chair."

I explain what happened in math class and
show her some of my bruises.

Doc's whiskers twitch when she winces.
"You should be angry
from all the bullying,
but I don't see you
expressing that emotion.
Come with me."

We go outside,
and Doc hands me a bottle of soda.
"Give it a good ol' shake."
I do, as I show her some side-eye.
"What's this all about?"

"Patience is a virtue."
Her rabbit nose makes her sound
as if she has a cold.

"Patience is a virtue, Doc,
but impatience is a gift.
And I'm gifted."

She laughs until she snorts,
sending the fake rabbit nose soaring,

while I keep shaking the bottle.
"Now open it, Ellie."
"But it'll go —"
"Humor me."
"Don't say I didn't warn you, Doc."

A frothy, fizzy fountain
spews all over us.

"That's a perfect example of
what happens when
you bottle up anger.
Whenever you do release it,
it's going to make a huge mess."

MISMATCHED

I spot Mrs. Pochon
wheeling a cart full of books
to the library.
"If that cart were a book character,
it'd be Cartniss Everdeen.
Quiet and stealthy," I say,
coming alongside her.

She laughs.
"You're so clever.
That reminds me.
I've been thinking
you'd make a great student assistant.
I could really use some help
shelving books and
creating displays.
You could pack your lunch and
eat in the library workroom.
Interested?"

Volunteering in the library
would keep me away from
Marissa and Kortnee in the cafeteria
  every day,
instead of just when I can slip away.

"I sure am!"

"I just ask that you always have
one display of new releases,
but I trust you to decide the other
  themes.
A few of the display areas
include bulletin boards.
Can you decorate them, too?"

"I have plenty of ideas, but
I'm not very good at drawing or art."

"No problem.
I know just the student
to pair with you."

The next day,
as I gather books about bullies,
in walks one:
Enemy Number 3.

PURE GARBAGE

"A wonderful writer teamed with
an amazing artist.
Together, you two can do great things,"
Mrs. Pochon says,
leaving us alone
to work on the bulletin board
and book display about bullies.

Enemy Number 3
scans the novels I've pulled.
"These are all about
people being bullied because
of how they look.
You know, people are bullied
for other reasons, too.
I know a book that'd be good."
He heads to the stacks and
comes back

to hand me one about a boy
who's made fun of because
of his family.

I tell him my idea.
"The focal point will be a trash can.
Then we can create
a pocket for blank index cards and
a pocket for index cards with
great quotes from books, such as
'I'm only different
to the people who see
with the wrong eyes'
from *Fish in a Tree*.
Then the bulletin board sign can say,
'Take out the garbage.
Stop junking up your mind with
stinky things bullies have said to you.
Toss them into the trash, then
pick up a good thought
to replace it.'
We could use bright colors,
draw people's attention."

"Maybe."
He stares at the bulletin board.

I know that look.
Viv gets it when she's brainstorming.
He grabs his sketch pad and
colored pencils,
draws for several minutes, and
then slides the sketch pad over to me.
He's used black, red, blue, and purple.
He's really good.
I'm impressed.

"Why those colors?"

"Bruises are purple.
Anger is red.
Sadness is blue."

"And the black?"

He starts sketching again.
"That's how you feel inside
when you've been bullied."

I don't even think
before I speak.
"How would you know
what it feels like to be bullied?
You *are* a bully."

His face turns red, as if
I've smacked him.

"You're not the only one
who doesn't fit in
around here, Splash,"
he mumbles as
he starts drawing and
cutting the construction paper.

Then I get it.
Enemy Number 3's not just a bully.
People bully him
because he's poor and
wears raggedy clothes.

But I just don't understand how
someone who's bullied
and knows how horrible it feels inside
turns around and bullies others.
That's pure garbage.

STUFFING

Catalina and I really want to go
  swimming —
it's now one of our favorite things
to do together —
but it's storming.
So we end up listening to music
in my room and
singing along using licorice
as microphones.

We've grown so close,
we also tell each other
almost everything.

I even told her about
my mom's obsession with inventorying
  food,
so now Catalina brings snacks
along with her guitar.

"I keep my backpack stocked," she says,
licking the spicy coating from her chips
off her fingers.
"Ugh.
Still red."
She heads to the bathroom
to wash her hands.

While she's gone,
I quickly stuff all the trash
in her backpack.
I know she'll
understand why
I did it.

No Mirrors

When someone comes to your house,
it's easy to forget that
what's normal to you
can seem so strange to others.

Catalina looks around my room.
"I just noticed something.
There's not a mirror anywhere."

"You wouldn't understand."

"I'm willing to try."
She sits crisscross applesauce
and strums her guitar softly,
like a soothing lullaby.

Maybe that's why I start talking.

First I bite into a marzipan,
and the crumbly, nutty candy
melts in my mouth like powdered sugar,

226

taking away some of the bitterness
I feel remembering the day
I took down the bathroom mirror.

"I haven't had a mirror since the day
my mom made me look into one
while she pointed out everything
wrong with my body."

I don't tell Catalina
what she actually said:
"Cellulite on your thighs.
Stretch marks on your arms.
Rolls of fat on your stomach.
Aren't you ashamed of yourself?"

Mirrors are heavier than they look.
When I tried to pry mine off the wall,
I dropped it.
Watched it shatter into a bazillion pieces.
I saw bits and pieces of me
in the shards.

And it hit me.
That's how people see me,
as bits and pieces of fat.
Not as a person.

MADDENING CYCLE

"Has your mom always been so
   terrible?"
Catalina asks.

I let out a sigh.
"She's obsessed with diets,
trying to find the magical one
that'll make me skinny.
She's got me on one now
— or *had* me on one."
I ball up the candy bar wrapper,
throw it at her, and grin.
"Sometimes I wonder why I even try.
I mean, I'm not even sure being fat
really bothers me.
How people treat me
because I'm fat bothers me."

"And her diets don't help?"

"Sometimes.
For a while.
But not really.
It's like I've gotten trapped in
this maddening cycle.
You're a little overweight as a kid.
People hurt your feelings about it.
You eat to bury the shame.
People hurt you more.
You eat more.
Infinite loop."

"Have you gotten teased
since you were little?"

"The word is *bullied*.
And yes.
People never leave me alone.
Not at school.
Not anywhere.
Not even at home.
I doubt it will ever stop."

"*That* is so maddening," Catalina says.
She reaches over and hugs me.
Just like Viv used to.

GETTING SOMEWHERE

I hand Doc a mini-coffin
when she wants to see my collection of
the hurtful words people say to me.

She turns the box over in her hands.
"That's where I keep the lists," I tell her.

"Well, I'll say this for ya.
You never fail to surprise me.
Why a casket?"

I could tell her because it was on
clearance after Halloween,
which it was,
but I tell her the whole truth.

"Journaling showed me
I bury my feelings,
so it seemed fitting."

She smiles.
"Now we're getting somewhere."

"I included the hurtful stuff
I say to me, too.
Fat Girl Rule:
You need to bully yourself
as much as,
if not more than,
everyone else bullies you."

"Tell me more
about the Fat Girl Rules," Doc says
as she flips through them.

"So these are the rules you live by?"
I nod.
"There sure are a lot of them, Ellie."
"And I add new ones all the time.
I used to think if I could just
follow the rules, then
people would stop
being mean to me.
But, duh, that didn't happen."

Doc asks to borrow the list
to look over all the rules.
I let her.
I have them memorized.

HAPPY BIRTHDAY TO ME

I know two things when
my parents hand me a
plane-shaped birthday card.
I'm going to visit Viv
over Thanksgiving break,
and Dad made it happen.

He throws his arms around me.
My dad gives the world's best hugs,
holding me without smothering
and filling me with
warmth and love.

I lightly hug Mom,
try to keep her from feeling my fat.
Our hugs are like
trying to make puzzle pieces fit
in the wrong places.

Mom pulls away.
"Now, Ellie, remember to —"
Dad clears his throat.
She sighs.
"To have a great time."

Away from her, I will.

FOOD BRINGS YOU TOGETHER

Catalina invites me to
an early Thanksgiving celebration
since her family's spending
the holiday in Mexico.

Relatives pack her house,
and I wish I could live in
her kitchen.
Catalina's mom and aunts
cook honey-baked ham,
chile-rubbed turkey with mole gravy,
tamales, tortillas,
corn bread with jalapeños,
rice and beans,
and other foods
I don't recognize,
which smell irresistible.
They switch languages,

sometimes mid-sentence,
from Spanish to English like
Bobeshi switched from
Hebrew to English with
Yiddish mixed in.

When it's mealtime,
it's like a game of musical chairs
as everyone scrambles for a seat.

Catalina's dad and abuelo
say prayers of thanks; then
everyone passes
bowls and platters around the table.

Once we fill our plates,
everyone starts
eating,
talking,
laughing.
And no one
watches what I eat.

The laughter grows after dinner
as we play games and
eat dessert:
pumpkin empanadas and flan.

I feel so happy and relaxed
as I return home.
How I feel after dinner at Catalina's
is so different from
how I feel after dinner at my house,
when I get muscle cramps from
drawing in my shoulders and legs
to try to take up less space and
make myself smaller.

I didn't need to do that today.

Catalina's family showed me
food can bring you together
instead of tear you apart.

And I'm thankful.

THANKSGIVING PRAYER

The first sign
our family Thanksgiving
is going to be a disaster
is when Liam
sticks a finger into one of the bowls and
scoops up a mouthful.
He quickly spits out the food.
"These potatoes are spoiled."

"It's mashed cauliflower,"
Mom says.
"Fewer carbs and calories.
And never put your finger in a bowl."

Dad passes the
platter of sliced turkey breast
around the table,
then a bowl of steamed Brussels sprouts
and the mashed cauliflower.

Mom had already dished up
what I'm allowed to eat,
so I stare at the cornucopia-shaped
salt and pepper shakers as
I wait for Dad to bless the meal.

And I say a Shakespeare-style silent
    prayer
under my breath
for an asteroid to hit.
O asteroid, asteroid.
Wherefore art thou, asteroid?

"So where's the rest of the meal?"
Liam searches the kitchen.
"The turkey legs?
Gravy?
Cranberry sauce?
Dressing?
Creamed corn?"

"All of that's fat,
carbs, and sugar."
Mom spears a sprout.

"So we can't even have
Thanksgiving like normal people anymore?

It's always all about Ellie.
I'm gonna go find some real food.
Maybe one of my friends
will take me in.
I'm outta here."

ODDS ARE

Like jumping in front of a
runaway train,
Dad stands up,
stops Liam in his tracks.

"Apologize to Ellie — now!"

Liam looks at me.
"Sorry we all have to suffer
because you're fat."

"Liam Isaac."

"Sorry you ruin everything."

"Liam Isaac Montgomery-Hofstein."

"Sorry you're my sister."

"That does it.
Give me your car keys."

Dad stretches out his right hand.
Liam digs through his pocket and
dangles the key ring midair.

"How long?"

"After you go two weeks
without insulting your sister.
One insult and
we start over with the count."

"That's not fair!"

"You're right.
Make it a month."

Liam has to go a month
without insulting me?
The odds are better
that the asteroid will hit.

AND WE HAVE TAKEOFF

Taxiing down the runway,
the seats shimmy
and the plane squeaks,
like driving a car quickly
down a bumpy road.

Soon the nose is in the air.
Thump goes the landing gear
as the wheels retract,
tucked back in like
a bird tucks its legs
during flight.

Everything that seems so
big and overwhelming,

like school and home,
suddenly grows small
and slowly disappears.

I'm free from it, for now.

Free as a bird.

STRETCHING

I have two seats,
so I starfish,
lean my head against the window,
lift the seat arm,
and stretch out my legs.

When my family flies on vacation,
I sit next to Dad.
He doesn't care if
my arms or legs touch his.
But since I'm flying alone,
I didn't want to sit next to
someone who might throw a fit
and say a fat girl's oozing onto their seat.

Aunt Zoey's been booted
off a flight, forced to
walk down the exit aisle
while everyone watched.

And I've heard about
social media posts from
passengers who hate
to sit next to fat people.
Dad has, too.
That's why he bought me two seats.

And I'm pretty sure
Mom doesn't know.

DOWN IN KOKOMO

"There's a beach song called 'Kokomo,'
but the only waves around here
are waves of corn and soybeans
and now they've all been harvested,"
Viv says.

We barely take a breath,
talking nonstop during the
hour-long car ride from Indy to Kokomo.

"Next time, I'm visiting in the summer."
I blow on my hands to defrost them.
"How does anyone live
in this cold?"

"Hot food does wonders,"
Sue says when we get to their house.
She scurries to the kitchen.
The sweet scent of

yeast rolls rising
tempts my taste buds
as she starts dinner.

I focus on a dry-erase board:
Good luck on your test today.
Love you, Mom.
Right back atcha, kiddo.
I read note after note.
And there's not a single article
about weight loss.

That's when I get an idea
for the refrigerator at home.

GROUNDHOG DAY

Before we go to bed,
snow like powdered sugar sprinkles
the trees.
By morning,
the branches sag under
six inches of snow
like thick vanilla icing on a cake.

"Whatcha wanna do today?" Viv asks.
"We have skis.
Wanna try them out?"

I try to imagine skiing and see
my legs ending up
twisted like a pretzel or
in the splits.
The only splits this girl wants to do
are banana splits.

I offer up another idea.
"Let's build a snow woman!"

Snow's not common in the Big D,
and this is the first real snow
for Viv in Indiana,
so it takes us a few tries
to figure out how
to pack the snow.

The middle ball ends up larger
than the base,
so our snow woman leans.

"She's imperfectly perfect, like us,"
I say as we add
the finishing touches.

Cold and wet,
we take refuge inside.
Viv heats up some tomato soup
and teaches me how to make
a mean grilled cheese and
hot chocolate from scratch.

We eat while we watch
an old movie, *Groundhog Day*.

Phil, the weatherman, has to relive
one day until he gets it right.
February is a little over two months
    away,
but I know I can't relive this day.

We got it right.

Play Ball

Basketball is to Indiana
as football is to Texas.

I get to watch Viv
in action as Comet.
She works the crowd,
directs the band using her tail,
tosses school T-shirts to fans,
and dances with the cheerleaders.

Sneakers squeak and
the ball thuds and
makes a high-pitched ring as
players run up and down the court.
We score.
They score.
We stay tied the whole game.
We go into overtime.
Double overtime.

With seven seconds on the clock,
a Comet steals the ball and
passes it to half-court.
A player shoots.
Swish!
Three points.
Nothing but net.

We win!
I'm hoarse by the end.
It's the perfect ending to
a perfect trip.

GET THE MESSAGE

Getting up early is worth it when
Mom walks into the kitchen
and sees the refrigerator door.

And all the cabinets.

I plastered articles like wallpaper
for Mom.

My faves:
Studies show a family's comments
about an overweight child
add to a negative self-image.

Studies show it's not just
kids and teachers at school
who make fun of overweight kids;
parents also bully them.

Kids don't need parents' judgment;
the world gives them plenty of that.

She doesn't say a word.
Maybe she got the message.

At my next appointment with Doc,
she asks for examples
of how I've been standing up
for myself lately.
I mention leaving articles for Mom.

"Genius idea!
The best way to be understood
is to learn and speak
someone's language.
So is she still
putting up articles?"

"She can't.
I put up articles.
Plastered them everywhere.
I've even started
tacking them to my parents' bedroom
    door."

WHAT DO I WANT?

The more someone gets to know you,
the scarier it can be.
"What'd you think?"
I ask when Doc gives me back
my list of Fat Girl Rules.

"It's not light bedtime reading,
that's for sure.
It seems like these rules
would make you think about
and hate your body
every minute of
every day."

"That's what society wants."

"What about what you want, Ellie?"

"No one's ever asked me."

"I just did."

I grab the throw pillow,
hold it in front of my belly,
slip my fingers through
the loops of the fringe
around the edges, and
twist the threads tight
until my fingers turn white.

"I want people to accept me,
just as I am."

"So who are you, Ellie?
Describe yourself without
talking about your size."

I hug the pillow
up higher,
near my heart.
"I can't."

Doc puts down her notepad.
"The problem with
the Fat Girl Rules is
you've let them not only
decide how you're going to live,
but also define who you are."

A CHANCE TO BE A BULLY

"I think we should try a little exercise,"
Doc says, and
taps an index finger to her lips.
"Which one?
Hmm. Hmm. Hmmmmmmmm."

"Just spill it.
Get it over with."
I hold the throw pillow
in front of my stomach again.

"You don't have to hide
any part of yourself," Doc says.
"I see all of you.
I accept all of you."

I freeze,
finally realizing why I hug pillows.
I put it down.

"How do you feel without it?" Doc asks.

"Vulnerable.
A little naked."

"Can you try it for a while,
see what happens?"

I nod.

"Good.
Have you ever dreamed
of being someone else?"
"Only every single day."
"Then today your dream comes true."
"I thought you were my therapist,
not my fairy godmother."
"What can I say?
I have a lot of hidden talents."

She jogs over to the art table,
dips her pen in glitter, and
spins around as she
waves it like a wand.

"Bibbidi-bobbidi-boo.
You're Marissa.
And I'm you."

I'm pretty sure Doc would have to
cut my heart out
for me to act like Marissa,
but I'll give it my best shot.

"You need to stuff this
under your shirt."
I toss her the throw pillow.

I stand up and
circle her chair so
I can look down on her.
One side of my upper lip
curls up as I focus on the
frumpy, clumpy, bumpy pillow.
"You're so fat
you make whales feel skinny."

"That's a really hurtful
thing to say."

"Well, it hurts my eyes
just looking at you."

"Why are you so mean to me?"

I bend down so
we're face-to-face.
"Because you deserve it."

DESERVE IT

Too bad magic isn't real;
you could fix everything
with a wave of a wand.

Doc waves her pen again.
"Bibbidi-bobbidi-boo.
Switcheroo.
Now I'm Marissa,
and you're you."

I sit in the chair.
Doc stands.
"You deserve to feel pain."
She's a better Marissa than I am.
She goes right for the jugular.
I'm a mini-marshmallow
in scalding hot chocolate,
melting fast.
Going —

Doc bends down and leans in
so we're face-to-face again.
"Admit it."

Going —

"Admit it!"

Gone.

I nod.

Doc pulls up a chair beside me.
No one looks down on anyone now.
"You don't stand up for yourself
because you think you deserve the hate."

I nod,
do an amazingly good impression
of a bobblehead.
"I'm fat.
I deserve whatever anyone
says or does to me."

"No, Ellie.
You don't.
No matter what you weigh,
you deserve for people to treat you
like a human being with feelings."

A lump grows in my throat, and
I think I can't breathe, but
I just can't swallow, so
I gasp in a gulp of air.

But I'm not,
I think.
I'm a big ol' fat thing.

My own mom said so.

WITH THE WAVE OF A WAND

Like Cinderella,
my magical time ends.
Doc's wand is a pen again,
poised to take notes.
"What we just did was role-playing,
which allows you to
think, see, and feel like
someone else and
see yourself through their eyes.
What did you learn from it?"

"That your impression of me
needs a lot of work."
She pretends to take
a knife out of her heart.
"And that I give bullies
way too much power.

They tell me
how I should see myself,
how I should feel about myself.
How do I change that?"

She grins from ear to ear.
"I'm so glad you asked."

Doc has two assignments for me.
The first is to tell Mom
when she hurts my feelings.
If I don't feel comfortable doing that
   alone,
I should ask Dad to be there with me.

The second assignment is
to start replacing all my
untrue, negative thoughts
with true, positive thoughts.

That reminds me of
what I have students doing with
the trash can bulletin board
Enemy Number 3 and I made
at the library.

But it's a lot easier
to toss into the trash the thoughts
others have about you
than the ones
you have about yourself.

Deep Doo-Doo

Thanks to a screwdriver and chutzpah,
I'm about to get some practice
with changing thoughts.

Every Monday, Mom makes me
step on the scale.
I'm eating breakfast when
she stomps into the kitchen.
"Where is it?"

"In the trash."
I eat the last spoonful of yogurt as
she digs through the garbage.
I buried all the pieces of
the scale on the bottom,
underneath dog doo I dumped.
She gets it all over her hands.

"You're grounded, young lady!"

Doc and I talked about
me having the right to stand up to Mom,
just like anybody else,
and that she probably wouldn't be happy
  about it.
Doc and I didn't talk about
involving dog poop.
Crappity crap crap.
My bad.

"What do you think you're doing?!"
She gags as she runs to the sink.

"Not letting you weigh me again."

Untrue, negative thought:
The higher my weight,
the lower my value.
True, positive thought:
A scale does not
determine my worth.

I'm Ellie

In English class,
Mrs. Boardman asks
us to sum up what we've read with
our favorite quotes from the book.

I know just the quote
from *Song for a Whale*.
I raise my hand and
she calls on me.
"The whale 'didn't need to be fixed.
He was the whale who
sang his own song.'
That really hit home.
That's what the best books do.
They make you think,
and rethink
how you see
yourself,

268

others,
and the world.
Most of all,
they make you feel.
Feelings toward people
who aren't like you.
Feelings you didn't know
you had."

Mrs. Boardman asks me for an example
of singing your own song.

"Well, a lot of people blindly follow others
instead of thinking for themselves,
having their own voice."
My eyes meet Kortnee's.
"It's okay to be different.
We're all different.
Inside, everyone just wants to be
accepted for who they are,
but then they act like other people
to fit in."

"What do you know?
You don't fit anywhere,"
Kortnee whispers.

I'm a whale,
and she's like a hunter
always ready to attack with
her harpoon tongue.

I think about what Doc said,
how I need to replace all my
untrue, negative thoughts with
true, positive thoughts.

So I say to myself,
I'm not a whale.
I'm Ellie.

BELONGING

"Hola," Sonya says,
opening the front door for me
and giving me a hug
when I arrive for a sleepover
a week later,
since I'm no longer grounded.
"Catalina's up in her room.
Hopefully, she's finished cleaning.
It was a mess."
She rolls her eyes and shakes her head.
"That girl.
What is it you say, Ellie?
'Oy vey'?"

We laugh.

"I'd better get back to the kitchen.
I'm making your favorite dinner.
Chicken enchiladas."

My mouth waters.
"Gracias!"

"Hey, hermana,"
Javier, Nat, and Izzy call out
from the great room as I start up the
  stairs.
"Hola," I say.

I'm over here so much,
we're family and
speak each other's language.
Belonging feels good.

"Looks nice," I say to Catalina, and
start to open the closet to
hang up my jacket.

"Stop! Don't!"
She throws her body across the door.
"I might have tossed stuff in there.
Possibly.
Maybe.
Just don't open it.
Unless you're wearing a helmet.
Or feeling lucky."

With the clutter gone,
I notice that in the middle of all the
   music posters
on the wall, there's a map
of Mexico before
the Mexican-American War.
It draws my attention like
a long dash in a sentence.

People make Catalina feel
unwelcome here,
but Texas belonged
to her family
long before mine,
long before the rest of us.

It's not fair.

Hanukkah Miracle

Catalina thinks Hanukkah is
the Jewish Christmas, so
before she joins us for Shabbat
during the Festival of Lights,
I enlighten her.

Neighbors gather in our
backyard as Dad babies the brisket
all day in the smoker.
He makes an extra one to share.
He talks tips and techniques,
but he won't share his recipe.

Barbecue is its own religion in Texas.

I'm just thankful
the Maccabees' miracle
involved oil so we can
feast on fried foods,

like potato latkes and
sufganiyot crammed
with blackberry jam.

The true Hanukkah miracle is
Mom not saying a word about calories.
I figure it's because of the articles
I've been leaving for her.

UNWRAPPED

Catalina and I exchange gifts
in the spirit of Christmukkah.

She opens hers first,
a leather journal with music
  paper
so she can write songs.

"I can't even begin to guess
what this is," I say,
peeling the paper off my present.
The box is taller than me and
so heavy she had to have Javier
carry it to my house.

"Side of beef,"
Liam mumbles when he walks by.

"New brother."
Catalina doesn't mumble.

"That would be such a miracle,"
I say.

"You wanna talk miracles?
Liam being nice — now, *that*
would be a miracle," Catalina says.
She turns to Liam and challenges him.
"Why don't you try it sometime?"

"Oh, I bet he's nice to her sometimes,"
  Javier says.
"He knows we're lucky to have sisters
to crack us up."

It's wild that Javier is so nice,
he can't imagine that Liam's so mean.

After Javier leaves,
Liam gives me an odd look,
and I wonder if he'll
ever see me like Catalina and Javier do.
I'm so focused on my thoughts,
I almost drop the box.

"Be careful."
Catalina holds the box steady
after it tips.
"It might break."

It does break.

My heart.

I run my fingers along
the Mexican punched tin and
orange-and-blue Talavera tiles
framing the full-length mirror.

I see me,
all of me,
for the first time
in a long time.

My brown, curly hair.
Milk-chocolate eyes.
Slightly tanned skin from swimming.
Apple cheeks.
Round, soft body.

I can't hold back the tears.

It's beautiful.

And I'm beautiful.

SERVING CHRISTMAS

Once a year,
we come together and
act like a real family
when we volunteer
to serve Christmas dinner
at the mission.

When we run out of cookies,
I go to the pantry for more.
I turn the corner and see Enemy
   Number 3.
He's trying on shoes.
When they fit perfectly,
his face lights up.

His mom points to a pair of pants
that are right in front of me.
I quickly turn the corner.
It's my turn to slam

my body against a wall
and suck in my stomach
to make room for him
so he doesn't know
I know where he gets his clothes.
He might not deserve that kindness,
but I know he needs it.

STARTING OVER

Mom has to work late,
so Dad and I get to make s'mores
in the chiminea.

I hold my toaster fork over the flame
until the fire chars it black before
I blow it out and eat it,
crunchy, sticky, and sweet.

On the patio table,
I see the latest book he's been reading.
"Is it any good?"

"It's very interesting,"
he says as he bites into a s'more
and strings of white goo
stick to his chin.
"It's about cultures that have
ceremonial burnings

to symbolize letting go and
starting over."

I know what I want
to let go of
so I can start over.

"Be right back."
I go to my room and return.

As page after page
turns to ash
and floats up the chimney,
I feel more and more free.

Fat Girl Rules
make for great kindling.
I've realized
it's the only thing
they're good for.

ALL FIGURED OUT

Doc starts with small talk
to get me talking, then
— boom —
catches me off guard
with a question.
I have her all figured out.

She asks what I did
over the holidays.

"I destroyed the Fat Girl Rules."
I reach for a throw pillow.
Put it in front of my stomach.
Quickly put it back down.

Habits are hard to break.

"Fat Girl Rules —
that's no way to live," Doc says.

"Tell me about it."

"So why did I hear a hint
of sadness in your voice
when you said you
destroyed them?"

As I think about Doc's question,
a memory comes to mind,
and I tell her about it.

"One time, PugsFurever rescued a dog
who'd spent her entire life in
a cage at a puppy mill.
Even after I opened the door,
she stayed inside the kennel.

"Every now and again
she'd stick out one paw or her head.
But then she'd look at the kennel,
all sad and a little afraid,
and slink back in.
Caged was the only life
she'd ever known.

"One day, two other rescues
scampered in and out of her cage.

They showed her they were free
and she could be.
She ran out and joined them.
I realized sometimes you need
someone who understands
what it's like to be bound
to show you how to be free."

ERASING THE BAD RULES

Doc and I agree
I'm a lot like the rescued pug.
I need to take some steps
to live like I'm free
from the Fat Girl Rules.

One of the steps is breaking free
from Mom's rules.
"Mom's always had
all of these rules.
Carbs are bad.
Fat is bad.
Snacks are bad.
So I've always felt like
food is bad
and
I'm bad
for eating

or wanting
or enjoying
or needing it."

Doc walks over and writes
Mom's food rules on a whiteboard
before sitting down.
"Your turn."

"All the rules are here.
What's left to do?"

"Just think about it.
It'll come to you."

I stand in front of the board
and read Mom's long list
of rules.

Then I grab the eraser
and get rid of
every
last
one.

Fix-Her-Upper

Mom's always finding new doctors
to take me to,
to fix me.

I'm Mom's fix-her-upper.

When she picks me up from school,
it's off to another appointment.
As she drives in the pouring rain,
I lean my head on the cool glass.
My puffs of breath fog up the window,
creating a writing surface.

Say you're ashamed of me, I think.
Say you're disgusted by me.
Say you'll never love me until I'm thin.

When we arrive at the doctor's office,
I slam the SUV door,
hoping she'll read the message
I wrote with my finger
on the fogged-up glass:
Just. Say. It.

A Big, Fat Surprise

We go to the doctor's office,
and he motions for us to have a seat
across from him.
Without so much as a hello,
he says bariatric surgery
is a growing option
for obese kids.

"A growing option —
that supposed to be punny?"
I cross my arms over my chest
to hide how much my hands
are shaking.

He smiles an awkward smile.
"Here's some information for you."
He slides a folder to
the edge of the desk,
inches from me,

right next to the plastic model of
a stomach and intestines.

This can't be happening,
but it is.

"So do you struggle to lose weight
and to keep it off?"
The doctor leans back
and clasps his hands behind his head.
His buttoned shirt gapes open,
stretched tight over his big stomach.

"Do you?"
I stare at his belly
like he's been staring at mine.

"Let's focus on you."
He explains the different surgeries,
benefits, risks, and side effects.
"Just think about it for now.
You could have a whole new life."

Or no life at all.

The doctor nudges the folder closer
    to me,
as if it's food I'll devour.

"Is that all?" I ask.

"Well, there are pre-op tests."

"So I do those tests and
then you slice and dice me?
Abracadabra,
I have a perfect life?
No more problems ever?
And Mom will finally love me?"

There, I said it.

I scoot to the edge of my seat
and wait for his answer.

Then Mom speaks.
"Ellie, we're just trying to fix you."
She places her hand on my shoulder.

And that's the final straw.

Blade Against Blubber

I knock the plastic stomach and
  intestines
off his desk.
My mind zeroes in on
the hated stomach,
the only part of me that matters to
  people.
No one cares about
my mind and its thoughts or
my heart and its feelings.

"Let's do this!"
I slam my hands on his desk.
"Where do I sign?
On second thought, why wait?"

I grab a pair of scissors
out of the doctor's desk caddy,
knocking everything off his desk.

Then I lift my shirt,
expose a roll of blubber,
and hold the blade against it.

"Eliana Elizabeth!"
Mom jumps up and
jerks the scissors out of my hand
as the doctor rolls his chair away from us.

"I think you'd better leave,
or I'll have to call security."

"Really, Doc?
Don't you want to
make — me — skinnnnnnny?!"

Mom tugs on my arm
to get me up,
forgetting how much I weigh.

I stand up,
smooth my clothes and hair.
"Nice meeting you."
I smown.

DUI OF ANGER

The drive home is pleasant.
Pleasant like stepping on
a Texas fire ant mound.
First comes a lot of fast biting and
   stinging.

"You embarrassed me to death!"
The tires squeal as Mom floors it
out of the parking garage.

"Yes. It's all about you,"
I say as she merges onto the freeway
and weaves in and out of traffic.
She's a maniac,
driving under the influence of anger.

"You completely overreacted."
She cuts off other drivers
and has honking contests.

"What I did was an *under*-reaction
after learning that
my mother planned for me
to have possibly life-ending surgery."

"Don't be so dramatic.
It's an option.
That's all I'm saying."

"Aunt Zoey almost died
from that same surgery."

"She was bigger than you.
More out of shape than you."
"So you hate looking at me so much
you're willing to chance
me dying on an operating table
or later from complications?"

Mom looks at me
instead of the road.
"I've never said I hate looking at you."

"DART bus!"
I scream, and point.
She swerves.

"You're out of control with your eating,
with that little episode back there."

"And you're a control freak.
Inventorying food.
Refusing to buy me clothes.
Trying to bribe me.
Or are we only allowed
to talk about my flaws?"

Fire ants' bites leave
swollen red spots
that turn into blisters,
making the pain last longer,
not unlike what we say to each other.

Mom turns onto our driveway
and jerks us both forward again
as she parks.
She throws her hands up in the air.
"I'm trying to help!"

"Yeah.
By so-called 'fixing me.'
Well, guess what?
I'm not broken!

And if I am,
it's because of you,
not my weight."

I slam the SUV door
and stomp to the house.

Not My First Rodeo

"Whoa!"
Dad says, using his firm rodeo voice
as if I'm a horse
out of control
when I slam the front door.
"Whatcha all bowed up about?"

"As if you don't know!"
I pound up the stairs.

Mom slams the front door.
"Get back down here, Eliana Elizabeth!"
She's ready for another go-around.

Bring. It. On.

"You Judased me, Dad!
You said you never would.
And you did."

"What in tarnation
are you talkin' about?" he says.
He looks at me, then Mom.
"Somebody'd better tell me
what's going on here."

Mom's motionless.
Quiet.

Then it hits me
like a big whiff of
fresh bull crap in an arena:
Dad doesn't know.
She's gone behind
both of our backs.

This ought to be good.

"How'd you see
all of this playing out, Mom?
Dad leaves for work one day,
you sneak me to the hospital,
I have weight-loss surgery,
and we're home by dinner?"

Dad jerks his head toward Mom,
who's staring at the floor.

"One thing Zayde taught me was
if a person can't look you in the eye,
you've got problems," Dad says.
"Big problems."

Mom folds her arms across her chest
and heads toward Dad's office,
her heels click-clicking.

He follows her,
then stops and looks up at me,
still frozen on the stairs.
"I'm so sorry, Ellie.
Truly, I am."
He slams his office door.

And their biggest fight ever begins.

WAVES OF EMOTION

"What's up?"
Doc leans in,
rests her elbows on her knees
and her chin in her hands.

"Mom took me to a doctor.
A bariatric surgeon."
I tell Doc everything.

"You're definitely a storyteller.
You described it perfectly.
But you're also a poet.
So tell me how it made you *feel*."

I shake my head.
"Facing feelings is like
swimming in a stormy ocean.
One wave of emotion hits and

then another and another until
I feel like I'm drowning."

"That's why you're going to learn
how to face each feeling as it comes.
So you just face one wave.
One wave at a time.
Not an ocean."

"Which wave first?"

"Well, you're a writer.
So let's start with a bunch of words.
Name all the feelings you have.
Then you can choose."
Doc throws open her arms.
"Toss 'em out.
No particular order."

I start slowly.
I think about the surgery,
being cut open.
"Scared."

I think about
Mom making me look in the mirror.
"Ugly."

Then the words come rapid-fire.
"Ashamed.
Embarrassed.
Mad."

"Good."
Doc takes notes.
"Let's dive deeper with one of those.
Give me synonyms for *mad*."

I clench my jaw. "Furious."
I raise my voice. "Livid."
I almost spit each syllable. "Seething."

I spring up off the couch.
Doc rolls back her chair.
Gives me space to pace
from one side of the room
to the other,
like doing laps in a pool.

SUPPOSED TO

My arms flail like
I'm swimming on land,
a fish out of water.

"To drag me in there like
I'm a freak of nature,
and want him to cut me,
slice me open,
rearrange and reattach organs
— just because of this."
I grab my stomach.
Shake it.
"It's not what a mom should do!"

I collapse onto the couch.
Hug the pillow to my chest,
hiding my heart,
not my stomach.

"Moms shouldn't do that."
Tears flow as I rock back and forth.
"She's supposed to love me."
My voice is a whisper.
"Just love me."

When I stop crying, the pillow's wet.
"I think I owe you a new one."

"Don't worry. I'll bill it to your mom."
Doc winks.
"You've come a long way."

"So no more sessions?"
I act like an excited puppy.

"But you'd miss me!" Doc says.

"Actually, I would," I admit.
"I like coming here.
You've really helped me.
I've learned a lot."

"It's important you learn
that not all doctors
are like the ones your mom's taken
   you to.
Try to find a doctor you like.

I'll explain to your parents why
it should be your choice;
they shouldn't have any say-so."

Mom with no say-so.
It's about time.

STRIKES ONE, TWO, THREE

Dad and I create a list
of the top ten doctors to try.

At the first appointment,
the nurse tsk-tsks
when she weighs me.
I turn around and leave.

At the second appointment,
with each pump of the black bulb,
the blood pressure cuff constricts my
   arm
like a hungry boa, until I think
my skin will burst open,
and my arm starts to bruise.
When I wince, the nurse says,
"Blame your big arm."
I scoot off the table and leave.

Dad calls her more prickly
than a West Texas cactus.

With the third appointment,
the doctor just stares at my stomach.
An octopus could be wrapped around
  my face
and he wouldn't see it.
I almost moon him,
to see if he'll notice that,
but my butt deserves better.
I slam the door as I leave.

FORGIVEN

When we get in Dad's pickup
after the third appointment,
he doesn't start the engine.
He cries.

I stare out the window as if
the orange wavy *W* of the Whataburger
sign nearby hypnotizes me.
I can't look at Dad when he's crying.
It'll make me cry.

"I'm so sorry, Ellie.
I wish I'd known your mom
was parading you around town
to doctor after doctor and
letting them treat you like this."

"I didn't want to cause
yet another fight by telling you
if you didn't know."

"Forgive me?"

I forgive Dad,
but it's Mom who needs to say
I'm sorry.

One Size Does Not Fit All

Doctors are like clothes.
One size does not fit all.
Not even close.
So I try on yet another one.

Regular and oversized chairs
fill the waiting room
so everyone can be comfortable.

"Want to know the number?"
the nurse asks as she weighs me.
I have a choice.
Power.
Rights.
Finally.
I shake my head.
"Okay, then, step on backward."

Dad makes lame jokes,
trying to ease the tension,
as we wait in the exam room.

After a gentle knock on the door,
it opens.
"Hi. You must be Ellie."
She looks me in the eyes.
Doesn't stare at my stomach.

So far, so good.

Speak Up, Buttercup

"As they say,
everything's bigger in Texas.
Six four.
And the weather up here's just fine,"
she says,
answering the questions
I'm not asking out loud.
"I'm Dr. Vasquez,
but most folks call me
Dr. V."

She isn't skinny,
but she's not obese.

"What brings you here today, Ellie?"
She sits down on the stool.

I swing my feet
dangling over the table
and search for the right words.

"Speak up, buttercup,
or I can't help you."

"I'm trying to find a doctor.
One who won't say,
'Looked in a mirror lately?'
Or, 'At least your parents
won't have to worry about
boys asking you out
in a few years.'
And if you mention bariatric surgery,
I'm leaving."

I don't mean to, but I cry.
Dr. V hands me a tissue.
"If all that happened to me,
I'd cry, too."

She talks all during the exam.
"Let me just tell ya,
I have sick patients of all sizes.
I have healthy patients of all sizes.
I'm not small,
but I take care of my body.
I get a checkup every six months.
I try to eat as healthy as I can,
minus chocolate because — hello —

what's life without chocolate,
and, okay, steak off the grill
because — hello — Texas.
I don't go to the gym,
but I contra dance, which is, well,
look it up when you get home."

She apologizes for the other doctors,
applauds me for my daily swims,
and treats me like I'm a person,
not a problem.

I make an appointment for
a six-month checkup with Dr. V
because — hello — I like her.

A Nice Moment with Mom

"Got a minute?"
Mom asks while
standing in my bedroom doorway.
She walks in before
I can even say yes.

What now?
My body tenses up, but
I scoot my schoolbooks over
so she can sit
on my bed.
Gigi's not about to budge, though.
This is her room
as much as it is mine.

"Dad tells me
you found a doctor you like."

"Yeah."
I hang my head down so
my hair drapes around my face,
a curtain to hide behind.
It's easier to say what you think
when you don't have to look at someone.
"I hated you dragging me
to all those doctors."

Mom takes a deep breath and
exhales it as a sigh.
"I shouldn't have done that.
It was a bad idea."

"Really bad,"
I add.

"So how are the appointments
with the therapist going?
Do you think she's helping?"

I nod.

Mom reaches over,
brushes the hair away
from my face,
gently cups my chin in one hand,

and lifts it
so we see eye to eye.
"I just want you to be okay.
That's all I've ever wanted."

I thought all you've ever wanted
was for me to lose weight,
I think.
I won't say it and
run the chance of
ruining the moment.
This is the kindest Mom has been since
— well —
I can't remember when.

And it's weird.
But nice.

ON THE RUN

Catalina is at the door,
talking so quickly and
crying so hard,
it takes several minutes for me
to understand what she's saying.

Somehow Gigi got out of the gate.
Catalina saw her chasing
the neighborhood squirrel.

"I ran after her.
She ran faster.
Thought it was a game.
I couldn't catch her.
I'm so sorry!"

I round up Anaïs and Dad.

Catalina recruits her family.

We divide up and
scour the neighborhood.

Catalina's family goes door-to-door.
Anaïs checks yards.
I jump in Dad's pickup.
With the windows down,
we coast around
block after block,
calling out Gigi's name and
stopping to look in bushes and culverts
and check around trash cans.

Hours later,
I'm no longer calling out her name,
just saying in between sobs,
"Gigi, please come home."

Gigi's gone,
but I'm lost.

Starfish in Distress

We give up the search
close to midnight.

"We'll find Gigi,"
Dad says,
giving me a hug
before going to bed.
"And then I'll make us
some soup
out of that stupid squirrel."

He's trying to help.
It's not working.

I can't sleep.
All night long,
I leave voice mails for
and send emails to
every shelter, rescue, and vet

I can find on the internet.
When the sun comes up,
I stare out my bedroom window,
hoping a bird's-eye view
will help me spot Gigi.
No use.

Exhausted, I collapse onto my bed.
I ball up,
a starfish curling in its feet,
showing signs of distress.

THE PLAN

I sit straight up when
I get the text.

Have your dog.
Come alone.

I don't recognize the cell number,
but I know that address.
It's just my luck that
the person who found **Gigi**
is someone who would
hold an innocent dog for ransom
just to be mean to me.

I will never understand
how some people can be
so cruel.

They have no right
to keep making my life miserable.
I have the power to stop this.
I come up with a plan.

HELD FOR RANSOM

I pound on the door.
Marissa opens it.

"Give me my dog."
Gigi's squirming.
I reach for her.

Kortnee blocks me.
"Not so fast."

Gigi whimpers.
Her tongue hangs out as she pants,
overheating from panic.

"Give. Me. My. Dog."

"She must be hangry,"
Marissa says.

"It just so happens
we have a snack."

Kortnee leaves and comes back to
  the door
holding a whale-shaped cake.

"Eat it," Marissa barks.
"All of it.
If you want your dog back."

I focus on Gigi.
"It's okay,"
I assure her.

"Yeah, it's okay, Gigi,"
Marissa says.
"As long as Splash
pays your ransom.
We're about to find out
just how much you're worth.
Eat the cake, blubberbelly."

Marissa swings Gigi by her harness.
She runs midair and
reverse-sneezes.
"What was *that*?"
Kortnee asks.
"Who knows."
Marissa rolls her eyes.

"It makes all kinds of weird noises.
Not unlike Splash over here.
Eat, disgusting whale.
Eat!"

Gigi doesn't take her eyes off me.
She trusts me.
Trusts me like I trust water.

I'd do anything for her.
Kortnee places the cake
in front of my mouth.

Marissa throws Gigi up in the air
and barely catches her before
she starts making a video
with her phone.

"I'm not going to eat that," I say.

"Splash says for the first time ever."
Marissa laughs.

"And I'm not going to let
either of you bully me ever again.
You two think you're better than me.
But you're just pathetic.
Look at all you did

to try to get at me.
All the time you spent planning this.
The money you forked over for the
  cake."
I laugh and lean in.
"But enough about you two.
Now give me my dog."

OUTNUMBERED

It all happens so fast.
Kortnee holds the cake closer to me.
I flip it back,
smashing cake all over her face.

Clumps of frosting fall off
and land on her feet.
She scoops away chunks
from her mouth and nose.
"I can't believe you did that!"

"I defended myself."
I close in on Marissa.
"I said, give me my dog."

"Make me.
It's two against one,
so you're out of luck,
loser."

"I think your math's off,"
Catalina says,
appearing all of a sudden
at my side.
"Looks like it's two against two."

"Three against two."
Anaïs shows up and locks arms with her.

"Six against two,"
Javier, Nat, and Izzy say.

CAPTURED ON VIDEO

Gigi covers me in kisses
all the way home.

"They didn't get the video
they'd planned on,
but I made a great one,"
Catalina says.
"Take a look."
It's short and shows
the cake
smashing against Kortnee's face.
It plays forward and backward.
Over and over.

I'm tempted to post it
on social media,
but that would be attacking
Marissa and Kortnee
and not defending myself.

So I just send it to Viv.
I'm pretty sure
I hear her laughing
clear from Indiana.

HASN'T HAD HER SHOTS

I tell Dad
Gigi needs to go to the vet.
"I don't think Marissa's had her shots."

The vet finds a small scratch on one eye,
probably from Gigi
crawling around bushes
as she chased the squirrel.
Eye drops will make it all better.
So, physically, she's okay.
Mentally, she's not.

When I go for a swim,
she-who-hates-water whines to join me.
She lies on my stomach as I float,
trusting me more than ever.

I feel guilty.

What happened to her
is my fault because I'm fat.

That's wrong thinking.
I replace that thought.

What happened to Gigi
was because Marissa and Kortnee
are mean girls.

BEHOLD THE THING

I'm sitting on my bed
with my back to the door
as I brush my hair.
The bristles hit
the mother of all tangles.
I wince.

"I can help."
Mom sits next to me.

I reluctantly hand her the brush.
She works one section at a time,
careful not to tug.
I close my eyes as the brush
massages my scalp.
Relaxing.
Soothing.

Comforting.
Words not usually associated with
  Mom.

"I didn't realize
how bad it was getting for you."

"The chair?
The photoshopped picture?
Those weren't clues?
And you see how I get treated —
sometimes you even blame me
for the way others treat me.
That's wrong, Mom.
But what's worse is
the way you treat me.
You can be my worst bully."

Mom hangs down her head.
"I realize now I've been saying
the wrong things.
I've always been better at writing
than talking.
I guess that's why
I like being a writer.

With writing, I can take the time
to find the right words
and not blurt out something
I might not even mean.
I've never been great at talking."

"No argument there."

Mom laughs.
"You're good with words.
Just be careful
to use them as tools,
not weapons."

I jump up.
"Great point, Mom!"
I look her in the eyes.
"You need to remember it, too.
Do you know what it feels like to
be called
a big ol' fat *thing*?"
I lean in.
"Thing!"
I say it softer.
Slower.

I pull away,
starfish,
make myself as big as I can.

"Take a good look, Mom."
I turn in a circle.
Once.
Twice.
Three times.
"Am I just a thing to you?
Behold the
thiiiiiiiiing!"

Mom buries her face in her hands.
"I'm sorry.
So very sorry.
Thing is a horrible word.
It should never be used
to describe any person.
I wish I could take back
ever saying that.
I honestly never meant to hurt you.
Ever."

I flop down on the bed,
exhausted.

I want to believe her,
but I can't trust her.

She tries to hug me,
but I jerk away.
The hurt's still too deep.

After Mom shuts the door behind her,
Gigi curls up against my neck,
and we both fall into a deep sleep.

PROUD OF ME

At my next session with Doc,
I tell her about Gigi and
standing up to Marissa and Kortnee.

"You defended yourself
without attacking them.
You did great!"

"And that's not all."
I give Doc
the play-by-play,
tell her how I confronted Mom.

When I get to the part about
"behold the thing,"
Doc stops taking notes,
slides one hand up
under her reading glasses,
and presses on her tear ducts.

"Just like that,
Mom wanted to hug me,
as if —"

"As if everything's fine now?"
Doc finishes my sentence.

I nod.
"I feel better, but not okay.
I think there's more
I want to say."

"We'll work on it."
Doc hands me a notebook
and tells me what to do.
"And, Ellie, I'm so proud of you."

If only Mom could say that.

I'm Ready

"Enough's enough."
Catalina stops strumming her guitar,
clunks it down on a patio chair,
jumps into the pool, and
puts her hand out like a stop sign.

I stop swimming laps.

"Spill it," she says
as we tread water.

I play stupid. "Spill what?"

"Don't even.
I know you.
Something's wrong.
You've hardly said a word in days.
Even though I have some
seriously mad conversation skills,
and can talk enough for the both of us,

343

I'm getting tired of hearing myself.
Speak."

For several minutes,
the only sound between us
is Gigi snoring, snuggled up
on my beach towel by the steps.

"Yikes!
It's something big, isn't it?"
Catalina swims closer to me.

I nod.
"My therapist wants me to confront
  Mom."

"Wowza!"

"I dread it."

"But you need to, Ellie.
You really do.
I don't know how
you've put up with it this long."

"What if it doesn't change anything?
What if it makes matters worse?"

"What if it helps?
What if things get better?"

I hadn't thought like that.
"You're right."

"I always am."

I laugh for the first time since
Doc told me I needed to confront Mom.

"How can I help?" Catalina asks.

"I need to figure out
what I'm going to say."

"Practice on me.
Pretend I'm your mom."

So that's what we do for days.
I rehearse my words with Catalina
during laps in the pool
and at night with Gigi,
who cocks her head
from side to side
listening to my every word.

I write them down, too,
in case I get all nervous and
forget what I want to say.

When the time comes,
I'm ready.

THIS IS MY TIME

Doc and I have company
for today's session.

Doc directs Dad and Mom
to two chairs not usually in the office.
Doc rolls her chair close to me.

"To be clear,
you're here
because Ellie asked you to come.
I'm here to provide any support
she needs to express her feelings
about things
that have happened,
about words
that have been said."

Dad and Mom nod in understanding.

"Ellie, whenever you're ready, begin."

I fold and unfold
the bullet-point list
of what I'd planned to say.

As I look over it,
I realize I've been
preparing for a trial,
offering up a defense
of why I should be loved.
I toss it into the trash.

I curl and uncurl
the throw pillow tassels
around my fingers.

"I don't feel like
you love me, Mom."

Mom leans forward,
starts to say something.
I stop her.

"No.
You've said enough.
This is my time to talk."

WEIGHT OF WORDS

I control my breathing,
like Doc and I
have been practicing.

"Mom, I don't feel like
you'll ever love me,
can ever love me,
unless
I lose weight."

I reach for a tissue
as the words catch in my throat.

"I used to think
I needed you to love me
or I would be
incomplete."

The tears flow.
I don't blink them back

or try to hide or bury them.
I take my time.
Feel them.
Each and every drop.

Feel them drain the pain.

When my tears taper off,
I look over at Doc.

"You're doing great.
Need to take a break?"

I shake my head.
Start again.
"I have people in my life
who love me,
so I'll be okay."
I smile at Dad.

He reaches for his bandanna
and dabs his eyes.

I clear my throat to make sure
Mom hears my final words.
"And I'm learning to love me.
The fat on my body
never felt as heavy as
your words on my heart."

I walk over to her
and place in her hands
a notebook full
of all the ugly words
she's ever said to me.

"It's time for you
to carry the weight."

She crumbles.

CATCHING A BREAK

Fun news.
Viv texts a photo of her with
sunshine-yellow hair striped with
orange rays.

Viv texts again.
Bad news.
Dad gets me for spring break.

And again.
Good news.
That means I get to visit you!

That's not good news,
I text.

What?!

That's the best news ever!

WHALING WALL

On the drive to pick up Viv
from her dad's place,
I spot something and
make Anaïs circle back.

Sometimes when you see
something all the time,
you forget it's there.
Like the Whaling Wall
in downtown Dallas,
an outdoor mural
featuring humpbacks.

I feel so small
looking up at them.
They swim.
They're smart.
They have huge hearts.
And they have a voice.

I've always hated
being called a whale,
but it's actually
a compliment.

They're big.
They're amazing creatures.
And they're beautiful.

Three Times the Fun

What's better than
a cannonball?
Three cannonballs.

Catalina gets an A
for originality.
She leaps into the air
and flaps her arms
like a newborn duckling,
its wings pretty much useless
for flight,
but at least it feels like
it's doing something
to try to save itself
as it falls.

Viv starts out well,
but lets go of her legs too soon

and ends up doing a
cannonball–belly flop.

Not to brag,
but I nail it.
Perfect form.

Perfect splash.

ROOM FOR STARFISH

I swim so often,
my two besties,
Viv and Catalina,
tucker out before I do.

I drift over to them,
and we stare at the sky,
the ocean of the heavens.

I tell Viv and Catalina
about starfishing,
how I'm not going to
try to hide myself
or make myself small anymore.

How I'm proud to be me
and to claim my right
to take up space.

I deserve to be seen.
To be noticed.
To be heard.
To be treated like a human.

I starfish.
There's plenty of room
for
each
and
every
one of us
in the world.

AUTHOR'S NOTE

Starfish is a work of fiction, and a lot of people will read this and think, "It's definitely fiction because people would never say or do such cruel things." But a variation of every single mean thing people said or did to Ellie happened to me when I was a child. Fat Girl Rules exist.

If you're being bullied, I understand what you're going through, and I care about you. You don't deserve it. Ever. No matter what.

Right now, many people still think it's okay to bully people who weigh more than they do. My hope is that *Starfish* will change people's attitudes and that, one day, no one will be bullied because of their size or for any reason. But until that day comes, know that no matter your size or who you are, you are lovable and deserve for people to treat you like you're a valuable person. Because you are.

ACKNOWLEDGMENTS

My dream of becoming a children's book writer came true with *Starfish*, and I have a lot of people to thank for their help along the way. You might recognize some of these names. I named characters after them as a way to honor them.

• God, for giving me the talent of writing so my voice can be heard

• Three very supportive people for all their prayers for me to get this book written, to find an agent, and to find just the right editor at the perfect house for me: my mom, Minnie; Richard Kiser; and Jeff Harlow

• The Society of Children's Book Writers and Illustrators for all their support of, and resources and opportunities for, writers and illustrators. Find out more about SCBWI at scbwi.org.

• The Highlights Foundation for the amazing workshops that helped me hone my skills: the Writers Workshop in Chautauqua; the Whole Novel workshop with Stephen Roxburgh; Novels in Verse workshop with Sonya Sones, Virginia Euwer Wolff, and Linda Oatman High; and the Master in Voice workshop with Patricia Lee Gauch. Find out more about the Highlights Foundation at highlightsfoundation.org.

• Stephen Roxburgh, former president of Books for Young Readers at Farrar, Straus and Giroux, who was the first to tell me I had what it took to write for children

• Author Sonya Sones, for becoming a true mentor and friend. *Starfish* came to me in free verse poems, but I'd never seen a book in a library or store written in free verse. So I kept trying to write *Starfish* in prose. Then, one day at a bookstore, I saw *Stop Pretending: What Happened When My Big Sister Went Crazy.* The title drew me to it. I opened it and read the first page. Sonya had written it in free verse. Not only is it one of my favorite books of all time, but Sonya opened a door for me that I never knew existed. It changed my life and my world.

• Patricia Lee Gauch, former editorial director of Philomel Books, for so freely sharing her years of wisdom, including to "go there," to write what's hard to even talk about

• My agent, Liza Fleissig, of Liza Royce Agency, LLC, for believing not only in my writing but also in me

• My editor, Nancy Paulsen, who's amazing beyond all measure and description. Originally, I wrote *Starfish* as a young adult novel. Nancy said I should rewrite it for middle grade because, as a YA novel, those who'd been bullied about their weight would read it and think, "Yep. That happened to me. It was horrible." But Nancy said if I rewrote *Starfish* as a middle-grade novel, I'd be able to reach kids while they're being bullied. I could help them realize their worth and give them the courage and tools they needed to confront the bullies. And maybe, just maybe, *Starfish* would reach the bullies and get them to stop. Nancy. Is. A. Genius. Pure. Genius.

• Sara LaFleur, associate editor, for teaching me so much about the editing and copyediting process

- Ryan Sullivan, copy editor, for your much-appreciated eagle eyes and expertise on the novel
- Jacqueline Hornberger, copy editor and proofreader, for your help on the author's note, acknowledgments, and first pass
- Cindy Howle, executive production editor, for making sure even the tiniest details were correct
- Designer Kelley Brady and Nancy Paulsen for so generously asking for my input on the cover at every stage of the process
- Illustrator Tara O'Brien, for her beautiful artwork. You totally captured the essence of not only Ellie, but also Gigi.
- Patricia Boardman, aka Peejer-Beejer, my junior high literature teacher and high school journalism teacher, who became my best friend, and who's always been my number one cheerleader
- Princess Gigi Pugsley, who was the best pug in the whole world. I'll never forget your love and antics. You saw me through some of the darkest days of my life. You were loyal and faithful to the end. Like Sonya Sones said when you

crossed the Rainbow Bridge, "Gigi will live on in your heart and in your poems."

• Joan C. Waghorn Pochon, former librarian at my elementary school, who always greeted me with a smile, recommended amazing books, asked my opinion about what I'd read, made me feel welcome, and helped me see libraries as a refuge from the world, especially when the bullying got to be too much — and to all the countless librarians around the world like her who make a difference every day

• Phil Montgomery, one of my favorite Texans, who gives life-changing great advice and counsel

• My writing critique groups in Texas and Indiana for the valuable input and encouragement — not to mention lots of laughter and friendship

• Indiana University for helping me translate English to Spanish

ABOUT THE AUTHOR

Lisa Fipps is a library marketing manager. *Starfish* is her debut novel. She lives in Kokomo, Indiana.